IN EARLY JUNE 1964,

the Benevolent Home for Necessitous Girls burns to the ground, and its vulnerable residents are thrust out into the world. The orphans, who know no other home, find their lives changed in an instant. Arrangements are made for the youngest residents, but the seven oldest girls are sent on their way with little more than a clue or two to their pasts and the hope of learning about the families they have never known. On their own for the first time in their lives, they are about to experience the world in ways they never imagined...

STONES ON A GRAVE

Kathy Kacer

ORCA BOOK PUBLISHERS

Library and Archives Canada Cataloguing in Publication

Kacer, Kathy, 1954–, author
Stones on a grave / Kathy Kacer.
(Secrets)

Issued in print, electronic and audio disc formats.
ISBN 978-1-4598-0659-7 (pbk.).—ISBN 978-1-4598-0660-3 (pdf).—
ISBN 978-1-4598-0661-0 (epub).—ISBN 978-1-4598-1090-7 (audio disc)

I. Title. II. Series: Secrets (Victoria, B.C.)
PS8571.A33S76 2015 jC813'.54 C2015-901747-5
C2015-901748-3 C2015-901749-1

First published in the United States, 2015
Library of Congress Control Number: 2015935516

Summary: In this YA novel, Sara arrives in Germany determined to explore her newly discovered Jewish heritage and solve the mystery of her parentage.

Orca Book Publishers is dedicated to preserving the environment and has printed this book on Forest Stewardship Council® certified paper.

Orca Book Publishers gratefully acknowledges the support for its publishing programs provided by the following agencies: the Government of Canada through the Canada Book Fund and the Canada Council for the Arts, and the Province of British Columbia through the BC Arts Council and the Book Publishing Tax Credit.

Cover design by Teresa Bubela
Cover images by Shutterstock.com and Dreamstime.com
Author photo by Nicole Kagan

ORCA BOOK PUBLISHERS
www.orcabook.com

Printed and bound in Canada.

18 17 16 15 • 4 3 2 1

For Zac, Jesse, Leila, Izzy and Zoe—
a new generation that will need to remember

One

THE SMOKE WAS choking Sara, sucking the air out of her lungs. It billowed in massive clouds from the orphanage roof, exploding like lava and pouring across the sky. Sara stood on the lawn facing the disintegrating building, shaking uncontrollably. She pulled a blanket around her shoulders, wondering briefly how it had gotten there. Had she grabbed it when she ran from her room? Everything was a blur. Who had awoken her, screaming in the middle of the night? She had a vague recollection of one of the girls—was it Toni?—pounding on her door and calling out frantically, "Fire! Sara! Dot! Tess! Get out of the house! Run! Ruuuunnn!"

Sara had staggered from her bed. She remembered clutching her roommate Dot's arm before scrambling down the long staircase, faltering in the dark.

They had practiced fire drills a thousand times in the past. But no one ever paid much attention. This was no rehearsal. This was real. Girls pushed up behind Sara as she stumbled against the ones in front.

"What about Tess?" Dot yelled.

"Not here." Sara had known without even checking that their roommate would not be in her bed. She would be out roaming, as she often did in the middle of the night.

No time to dress, Sara realized, glancing down at her nightgown and bare feet. No time to take anything, except the tin box under her bed. It held all the money she had been saving. She didn't even know how much was there—had resisted the urge to count it these last couple of years. She was waiting for a special occasion, maybe her birthday, to see how much she had saved.

If you ever had to leave this place, what would be the one thing you would take with you? Dot had once asked.

This box! Sara clutched it to her body and gagged, struggling to find a taste of something clean in the sooty night air.

"Are all the girls out of the house?" Mrs. Hazelton, their matron, was pacing, her eyes scanning the lawn where the girls were huddled in twos and threes.

She too was wrapped in a blanket; her hair, usually so neat, was wildly disheveled. This was the first time Sara had ever seen the administrator of the orphanage in a nightgown. Mrs. Hazelton was always so well-groomed, so perfectly put together. Sara couldn't even imagine the woman actually sleeping!

"Don't you worry, ma'am, everyone's out." It was Joe who responded. Their cook held two of the littlest girls in his arms. Their faces were buried in his shoulder. Sara watched their bodies writhe and tremble against his chest. "I'm countin' them all, just to make sure. And Miz Webster is here too." Their home economics teacher lived on the first floor of the house. "She's got a couple of the young ones with her—Donna and Jen."

Sara was counting as well. First the Seven. They were always called the Seven: herself, Toni, Betty, Dot, Malou, Cady and Tess, who had now mysteriously appeared, fully clothed, along with the younger girls. Were they all there? It would be okay as long as everyone was there. *Please be there!*

Others were gathering on the lawn—townspeople who usually kept their distance from the orphans. But now they looked concerned. They moved in between the girls, handing out blankets. Perhaps that's how Sara's had found its way around her shoulders.

She searched the crowd for a sign of Luke but couldn't see him. Did he even know what was happening? Would he come if he did know? Sara pushed that thought away.

"He's not coming, you know." Dot was standing next to her, holding little Debbie in her arms, a sobbing bundle of tangled hair and twitching limbs. Dot could always guess what Sara was thinking. "I keep telling you, he could care less."

Sara shook her head. It was true that her boyfriend didn't have the best reputation in town. But deep down she'd always believed that he cared—more than that: he loved her, even though it was hard at times to explain that to her roommate. "He probably doesn't know about the fire, or he'd be here for sure," she shouted back to Dot. That was it. Luke just hadn't heard yet.

"Are the fire engines coming? Can you see them?" Toni called out, always anxious, plagued with nightmares. Her face was silhouetted against the sky. Only a sliver of a moon still glowed above, disappearing in and out of the billows of smoke. What time was it? Two o'clock? Perhaps three?

"They're coming. I can hear them coming," Betty replied, calmly, protectively.

"Are they coming?" Toni repeated, eyes wide, shaking.

"Joe said they were on their way," Sara heard herself call out above the other cries, though she felt disconnected from her response. She was trying to keep her voice even. Maybe that would help still Toni and the others. But Sara's heart was galloping, and her breath came in shallow gasps. She clasped her hands together and rubbed them hard—a nervous habit. If she wasn't careful, she would rub them raw.

And the smoke kept pouring out of the building. It didn't help that the stench was nearly as suffocating. Acrid, sour, foul—like the burned dinner that Joe had served up a week earlier, but multiplied by a thousand, tens of thousands. The flames were next, breaking through the back part of the house where the rooms were—her room—and arcing up into the blackened sky. And the sounds! Who knew a fire could be so noisy—metal twisting and melting, wood crumbling—a cacophony of noises reaching a deafening crescendo. It howled like someone gone mad, pounding inside Sara's head.

"Are you all right, dear?"

Sara, startled, looked into the eyes of an elderly woman who had appeared with the other folks from town. She nodded, not trusting herself to speak.

"The building was old and run-down. Everyone knew that," the woman continued, shouting above the sound of crackling timber. "This was bound to happen."

Sara nodded again. *What are we going to do? Where was Luke?*

"You're not hurt?"

Sara shook her head. *Not in any way you can see.*

"It's just a building," the woman said. "So old and rickety. It's a wonder this didn't happen years ago. Glad everyone's out. That's the most important thing."

Sara nodded. Still no words. It's not just a building, she thought, defiantly—and sadly. It's my home—our home. And it's disappearing.

She clutched her tin of money closer to her chest and glanced back at the house just as the sign above the doorway—*The Benevolent Home for Necessitous Girls*—began to crumble. And then, in front of her eyes, it disintegrated, letter by letter, and tumbled to the ground, the pieces floating almost in slow motion, held aloft by a spring wind that whipped across the lawn.

"Stand back!" Malou shouted.

"I'm scared!" cried Dot.

"Hold on to someone." This came from Cady.

A fireball exploded high in the sky. Toni screamed and bolted for the river. Betty tried to go after her, but two of the younger girls were clinging to her as well, laminated against her legs.

And then, in the sudden stillness after the blast, Mrs. Hazelton's voice reached out into the night air, singing, "*Amazing grace! How sweet the sound...*" Others joined in. "*That saved a wretch like me...*"

Sara stood stunned and out of breath. *What's going to happen to us? Where will we go?*

"Stand back, everyone," Joe shouted. "It's comin' down."

Two

THE FIREFIGHTERS DID eventually arrive. They trained their hoses on what was left of the building, blasting it with jets of water. Pieces of wood, glass and siding hung suspended by the force of the liquid spewing from the fire-engine hoses and then eventually thudded to the ground. Sections of the house lay smoldering in unrecognizable piles. Sara remained speechless as she watched the building crumble. The sky turned from black to gray to hazy blue as dawn approached.

When it appeared that the worst of the fire was over, the girls turned to one another, not sure what to do next. After her burst of hymn singing, Mrs. Hazelton, usually so in command and full of orders, had become almost mute.

"How could this have happened?" she muttered, staring at the space that had once held the home she had presided over for years.

"Mrs. Hazelton?" Sara found her voice again and approached the matron to stand in front of her. At first, she didn't seem to be aware of Sara's presence. "Mrs. Hazelton," Sara repeated.

"What? Oh, Sara. Where are the others? Is everyone here?"

"Yes, we're all fine. A couple of girls inhaled a bit of smoke. But other than that, everyone is okay. And you?"

Mrs. Hazelton's gaze came back to rest on Sara. "What? Oh yes, I'm fine, dear, fine."

That was a lie, Sara knew. This place was as much Mrs. Hazelton's as it was the orphans'—probably more so! No one was going to be fine after this. Sara waited another moment. She could feel the other girls lining up behind her, also waiting. For what? Instructions? Reassurance? A bit of both, perhaps. Sara took another step forward. At eighteen, she was the oldest of the bunch—perhaps by just a few months, but even that meant something. Like the twin who always talks about being first, if only by minutes, it was time for her to act like the oldest.

"I think we're going to have to figure out what we're going to do now."

But before she could say another word, the townspeople took over. Someone grabbed Mrs. Hazelton by the arm and led her away. Someone else told the girls to get into waiting cars so they could be driven to the church. It was there that six of the seven girls who had shared a space in the orphanage for as long as they could remember were sprawled across wooden pews in the chapel and trying to settle in for a few hours of rest. Toni had not reappeared after her sprint to the river. No one was particularly worried about that, not even Betty. Toni was a wanderer and had stayed out until dawn many times, especially when she was anxious about something. Sara knew she was bound to reappear when things settled down.

A few of the younger orphans were scattered here and there. Most of them had cried themselves to sleep. But the older girls were still awake, staring at one another over the wooden benches, propped up by pillows and more blankets. Sara sipped a cup of tea that had been handed to her by another mysterious pair of helping hands. She wondered where these people had been over the years. *Funny how no one from town has ever paid much attention to us,* Sara thought. Some of them had openly showed their contempt—*like it's our fault our parents abandoned us.* None of that made sense to Sara. But now everyone was tripping over themselves to help. Disasters did that, she figured.

No one said a word. Each girl seemed lost in her own thoughts. Sara wanted to speak up; she wanted to say something wise and reassuring. She may have kept to herself a lot of the time, but she cared deeply about the others. After all, she had lived next to these girls ever since she had been brought to the orphanage as a baby. Her whole lifetime. She knew these girls like she knew herself; she understood their moods and dispositions. She knew that Betty was gentle and trusting and that Toni was scarred and haunted by nightmares. She knew that Tess was itching to get away from everyone and would be on the prowl as soon as she could get out. She understood that Malou was everyone's favorite, and Cady was usually distant and impatient. And she knew that even though she and Dot were almost the same age, Dot appeared to be so much younger. Sara wanted to say something to each of them, to tell them that she understood how they must be feeling and that she was feeling the same way. She wanted to let everyone know that they would be fine. But she barely believed that. She had no words. They had disappeared into some black hole in her head.

Miss Webster appeared, drifting into the chapel from another room. Sara noted the deep lines around their teacher's eyes and across her brow. Her face was pale despite the presence of two round dots of rouge that she had applied to her cheeks. Reverend Messervey stood behind her, there to make sure everyone was settled in for what was left of the night. Miss Webster was dressed, and her hair was combed into place. *Your first impression is what counts*, she always told the girls. She would never have wanted to look frazzled for too long.

"Girls, may I have your attention." Miss Webster spoke softly, peering around at the younger children, whose snores and soft breaths rose and fell in the church sanctuary. The six older girls sat up, instantly alert. "I know this is a shock for all of you—for all of us. For now, I want all of you to try and get some sleep." When Miss Webster spoke, she had this habit of waving her finger in the air, weaving it up and around like the baton that the music teacher, Mr. Rainey, used when he conducted the choir at the orphanage.

"Where's Mrs. Hazelton? Is she all right?" Sara asked. She knew it was a question that was on everyone's mind.

"The matron is fine. Don't any of you worry about that," Miss Webster replied. "She's gone back to her cottage to rest, which is what all of you should be doing as well." The cottage next to the Benevolent Home was where Mrs. Hazelton lived. Sara knew that it hadn't been touched by the fire.

"What's going to happen to us? I mean, we can't stay here in the church, can we?" Dot asked the question that Sara had been thinking.

"Here's what I can tell you for now," Miss Webster continued. "The fire has pretty much destroyed the house. It's burned almost to the ground, and it's not possible for any of you—any of us—to go back there." Murmurs exploded from the girls. Miss Webster's finger stopped in midair as she raised her hands to command silence. "Yes, it's not what we expected. But all of you know that the Home has been in the process of closing down for some time." Her finger resumed conducting.

That part Sara knew to be true. More and more of the younger children had left the Benevolent Home for Necessitous Girls in the preceding four years, adopted out to families who were eager to take a young child into their care. Now, in 1964, the Home, like other orphanages across the province, was being scaled down, phased out, closed. They were going the way of the Woodward's eagle—extinct!

Sara smiled in spite of herself. Of all things to remember at this moment. She had learned that bit of irrelevant information from the strange teacher who had drifted through town to give lessons to the girls on bird-watching—one of many instructors who had come for a short time and then moved on. What good would that piece of information do her in her life, Sara had wondered. But somehow, she had retained it.

"Nobody cares about what's going to happen to us. We were too old to give away when the orphanage started to close down, and we're even older now." This comment came from Cady—always sounding so annoyed.

Sara understood the irritation that burned inside of Cady. Sara's stomach also blistered at times, but not from anger. Sara felt a constant, creeping anxiety that nestled under her skin and festered there, like food gone bad or an infected scrape. It wasn't like Toni's anxiety. Toni was paralyzed with fear as obvious as a bad hairdo. Sara kept hers inside—concealed it with a smile and a nod of her head. Only her hands gave it away, rubbing together when she was agitated. And if she ignored the burn in her belly, it sometimes disappeared or settled into the background. If provoked, the feeling only got worse. That was how Sara felt a lot of the time, like a mosquito bite begging to be scratched.

"We all know that the house has needed some fixing for years," Miss Webster continued.

That's an understatement if there ever was one, thought Sara. Pipes leaked, lights flickered and went out, the old furnace banged and popped, sometimes so loudly that it woke the girls in the middle of the night. Was that why the fire had started? Because the house was so run-down?

"And Mrs. Hazelton has told me that the founders of the Home have had fewer funds to support us these past years." Miss Webster paused. "But she assures me that decisions are being made, and that she will be working to prepare for you as best she can." Her finger rose and fell in sync with that statement.

What did that mean? Preparing how? Sara had watched the younger girls leave, one by one, over the last few years. She'd known that after they turned eighteen, she and the other girls would also have to go. And she'd known, as Miss Webster had pointed out, that the home was slowly being phased out. But she had pushed those realities far into the back of her mind. The fire had brought what had seemed only probable into the realm of absolutely necessary. But there was another problem here, one that Cady had already alluded to. The girls who had left the orphanage for homes in other cities and towns were the Little Ones—the wanted ones, as Sara called them. No one wanted the Seven—too old to be welcomed as daughters for a newly married couple, but too young to be on their own.

Sara harbored a secret fantasy that the Seven would stay together forever, though that was something she had never said aloud. Sometimes, she even imagined that Mrs. Hazelton would be the one who would look after them, as she had been doing all these years. Everything was changing, Sara realized. None of it felt good.

As if reading her mind, Miss Webster gazed at the girls, taking them in one by one. "That's all I can say for now. I don't know much more than you do." Her voice was tired. Sara realized that Miss Webster was just as homeless as the rest of them. "Now is the time to sleep—even if it's only for a short time. In a few hours, Mrs. Hazelton will want to have a conversation with each of you. There are important things to talk about." She stopped there, letting her words and her waving finger hang in the air and settle on each of the girls. Sara, her body dead tired, looked up. She was about to open her mouth to ask for more details when Miss Webster spoke again.

"Don't even ask me any more questions. Rest. This is the start of a new day and a new time. We're all safe. That's what's most important." With that, she turned and left the chapel. The girls looked at one another.

"I don't like the sound of that," Dot said.

Betty was the one who replied. “Let’s just try and get some sleep. We won’t have any answers now, so we might as well do as Miss Webster says.”

Sara settled back down onto the pew, reached for her tin of money and stared into the darkened chapel. There was still no sign of Luke. Did he even care that she had just survived a fire?

Three

THOUGH LORETTA'S WAS usually closed on Sundays—the Lord's Day—Mrs. Clifford, the owner of the diner, had let it be known that she was going to open up this one time, so that folks who had helped out with the fire could come by for a meal. Even Reverend Messervey had given his blessing to the Sunday opening. And nothing, not even the destruction of the orphanage, stopped Sara from showing up at Loretta's on time the next morning. She had started working at the diner when she was sixteen. Mrs. Hazelton hadn't objected to her desire to get some work in town. As long as Sara kept up with her studies and chores at the orphanage, and didn't get home too late, it was fine with the matron. Sara bicycled into town to Loretta's four times a week, on the old rickety bike that Ed Sparling, the orphanage's handyman, tried to keep oiled and working. And every morning, her route took her past the welcome sign leading into town that read:

Hope

Population: 1,428

It was such a ridiculous name for a town that never seemed to change, neither moving forward nor back. Hope was small and insignificant and would probably always stay that way. Sara had never felt particularly attached to the town, and she certainly had never felt inspired by its name.

She parked her bicycle behind the diner and entered through the back door. Even the milkman was helping out on this Sunday and had already been there with his usual 6:00 AM delivery. Sara lugged the heavy glass bottles inside and paused in front of the mirror that hung next to the walk-in refrigerator, inspecting herself. Her steely blue eyes, like two round spots of crystal-clear sky, reflected back, looking weary from lack of sleep and the worry about her future that shrouded her. She grimaced. No way to get rid of the apprehension, but she had to do something to pull herself together before customers started to arrive. She'd simply fall apart—or snap—if anyone asked her any questions about the fire. She pulled her long dark curls into a ponytail and applied a thin layer of pink lipstick, rubbing her lips back and forth to move the color around. Then she added a couple of dabs to her cheeks, smoothing out the color with her fingers and pinching the apples of her cheeks for good measure. She stood back and inspected herself once more. *Better!*

Next, Sara stored the milk bottles inside the refrigerator and entered the dining area, flipping on the lights beside the door. The neon sign behind the counter snapped and buzzed a couple of times before the name—*Loretta's*—burst into pink fluorescent light. No one knew why the diner was called Loretta's or, for that matter, who Loretta was. That was just the name it had always had.

It was Loretta's when I bought it thirty years ago, and I've kept it that way ever since, Mrs. Clifford always said. *Why mess with something that works?* It was a popular stop for townsfolk and people passing through.

Sara moved around the diner, setting the chairs down from the tops of tables and filling the sugar jars and salt and pepper shakers. Had Mrs. Clifford felt sorry for her? Sara wondered briefly. Is that why she had hired her two years earlier? Whatever her reason, Mrs. Clifford was a fair and generous boss, and Sara tried hard not to take advantage of that. That's why she had arrived that morning to help open up.

Mrs. Clifford was surprised to see her. "You don't have to be here today, Sara," she said when she walked in an hour after Sara's arrival. She clucked sympathetically as Sara briefly described the fire.

Mrs. Clifford was a tiny wisp of a woman, barely reaching Sara's shoulder. Her age was a mystery to everyone in town. "I'll manage fine if you want to take some time," she continued, peering up at Sara from behind her oversized black horn-rimmed glasses. "Rest up for a few days. It must be a shock to lose that home of yours."

This kind of scrutiny was what Sara had dreaded. The word *shock* cut deeply into her, and she swallowed hard before replying. "It's okay, ma'am. I like being here. It helps clear my head."

That part was true. Anything that kept her busy would help keep her mind off her anxiety about what was going to happen to her and the other girls. It had been her last thought before she finally drifted off for a few hours of sleep at the church and her first thought as she awoke. Working at Loretta's was a great distraction. And she was proud of her ability to earn an income. She had been squirreling away her wages ever since she got this job—planning for a future that she hadn't yet figured out. All she knew was that it made her feel as if she didn't always have to depend on others. And that was enough for now.

In the early hours of the morning in the chapel, after all the other girls were asleep, Sara had pulled out her tin box, opened it and finally counted the money she had collected. Her wages were good—almost a dollar an hour. And the tips were pretty good too, especially when Mrs. Clifford had her work the dinner shift. Just a week earlier, Dr. Blunt and his wife had been in to celebrate their twenty-fifth anniversary. They had felt particularly generous and left Sara a whole dollar! That wasn't always the case; mostly, the customers left ten-cent tips, sometimes a quarter. Still, Sara knew that the money had to have added up over the two years that she had worked. But she never imagined how much was actually there—close to three hundred dollars. A fortune! The money was burning a hole in her pocket right now. It was one thing to keep it under her bed in the orphanage and know that no one would ever touch it. The church, even though everyone called it the House of God, was unknown territory. She hadn't wanted to leave it where a stranger wandering through might get his or her hands on it.

The door opened with a soft jingle from the bell above it, announcing someone's arrival. Sara quickly adjusted the apron around her waist. She was wearing a blouse and skirt that a woman at the church had given her the night before. The shirt was a bit snug, and she pulled self-consciously at the front of it, trying to get it to close over the skimpy bra that had been a donation from Guthrie's Bridal and Delicates shop. She couldn't complain though. All the girls' clothing had been lost in the fire. At least she'd had something to put on, not just the nightgown in which she had fled from the burning building. But she wished there was a sewing machine somewhere that she could get her hands on. The one from the orphanage was gone, along with all the material that had been stored in the common room. Give her a piece of fabric and she could create instant fashion. She dreamed one day of being a great designer like Mary Quant, who had just introduced the miniskirt. Sara even fantasized now and then that Coco Chanel might have been her real mother—well, perhaps her grandmother or great-grandmother, since the famous fashion designer was probably over eighty years old! All the magazines wrote about Chanel's ambition and the fact that both of her parents had died when she was only twelve, making her a young orphan like Sara. It never stopped Chanel from pursuing her passion. Sara had all kinds of ideas for designs. What was going to happen to those dreams now?

She looked up to see Luke enter the diner. He ambled over to the counter and sat down right in front of her, reaching across to nuzzle her cheek. Sara shrugged him away, glancing over her shoulder to see if Mrs. Clifford was watching. A troublesome feeling started to build in the pit of her stomach. She was still upset that Luke hadn't shown up at the fire or at the church. Should she say something? She wanted to, but...

"Hey, you're looking good." Luke checked out her too-tight blouse, letting his eyes rest a bit too long on her chest and on the lacy bra that was peeking through. She pulled on the front of her shirt again, her face burning, and then reached behind her to fill a cup with coffee, setting it down in front of Luke.

"I heard about the fire."

So, he did know. That made it almost worse that he hadn't shown up.

"I figured you were all okay," he said. He pulled a cigarette from behind his ear and dug in his jacket for a lighter. Sara grabbed the cigarette from his mouth and crushed it in a nearby ashtray, trying to make light of the gesture. Luke knew how much she hated cigarettes. But today, just a few hours after the fire that had destroyed her home, the smell of the smoke would have made her gag. Why didn't he think of that? she wondered.

Sara often asked herself what it was she saw in Luke—what kind of spell he had cast over her a few months earlier when he crawled out from under the truck he was repairing at the garage where he worked. Sara had biked there that day to get some air for her tires. She had seen him around town and had secretly taken pleasure in his dark good looks and the muscles that bulged under his tight T-shirts. He was a total hunk, just like Elvis, but even more dangerous. But that day he'd noticed her too, and said that he loved her dark curly hair and blue eyes. "Like Elizabeth Taylor," he said. "Better than all those blondies I see around here."

Few people ever paid attention to Sara's looks. And while she knew she couldn't come close to resembling the famous actress, she fell hard for Luke's smooth talk. But beyond being smitten by looks, and his attraction to her, what was there that drew her to him? Betty and Dot always told her that Luke was trouble. And Mrs. Clifford made no secret of the fact that she didn't care for him. But Sara knew it was a waste of breath to try to explain how it felt to be with Luke. How it felt to find a hand on top of hers or an arm around her shoulder. To be kissed on the neck and have soft words whispered in her ear. To feel beautiful and prized when she was with him. Yes, that was it. No one before Luke had ever really noticed her, let alone adored her. Sara had simply closed her ears to those who warned her about him. She'd heard only Luke's voice. And when he said he loved her, she could have melted away.

"You weren't involved with that fire over at the orphanage, were you, Luke?" Mrs. Clifford walked over to stand behind the counter next to Sara.

Luke cocked his head to one side and looked at Mrs. Clifford, a slow smile spreading across his face. "Now, why would you think I had anything to do with that?" he asked.

Luke and Mrs. Clifford stared one another down. "I've noticed that when there's trouble in town, it seems to have your name on it," she finally said.

"Those are all lies, Mrs. C. Ask Sara here. I'm an honest guy, right, baby?"

Sara felt her cheeks redden. Instinctively, her hands found one another and began to rub together. But before she could say a word, Mrs. Clifford continued.

"I heard you were bothering one of the girls from the orphanage yesterday—the colored one."

What? Sara quickly raised her eyes. Mrs. Clifford had to be talking about Malou, the youngest of the Seven and the most exotic, her skin the color of chocolate milk. Even Sara had heard the rumors that Luke and his pals sometimes went after Malou, calling her names and bothering her. Sara couldn't believe—wouldn't believe—the rumors were true. And Malou had never said a word to her.

"At the drugstore, I heard you were badgering that poor little girl. Mr. Pitt at the pharmacy saw it all. And it wasn't the first time either," Mrs. Clifford said.

By now, Sara's face burned brightly. Her hands moved across one another as if she were trying to start a fire with a stick of wood and a piece of flint. She longed for this conversation to end.

"More lies, Mrs. C.," Luke replied easily. "I'm just a hard-working guy. I've got no time to mess around like that."

Mrs. Clifford glanced from Luke to Sara. Then, with a loud snort, she turned and walked into the storage room. Luke snickered under his breath. "Now, where were we?" He reached over and pulled Sara toward him, jamming her hips up against the counter. Then he kissed her hard on the lips. He hadn't shaved that morning, and the rough stubble on his chin was like sandpaper against her cheek. She could taste the cigarette on his breath. Again, she pushed him away.

"Stop! Mrs. Clifford might come back." One of the buttons on her blouse had popped open, and she turned away from Luke, struggling to readjust her clothing.

"So what? You're my girl, aren't you? What's the problem?"

Sara finally secured the button and turned back. "It's not true, is it?" she asked carefully. "The stuff that Mrs. Clifford said about you...and Malou?"

Just then the doorbell jingled again. Sara turned away to try and get her breathing in check. Her hands shook as she put another pot of coffee on. Luke was drumming some kind of rhythm on the counter behind her.

"Hey, Sara," he said, his voice as smooth as velvet. "Looks like you've got a little friend come to visit. A dark shadow. With a curse on her."

Sara whipped around to see Malou standing at the entrance to the diner. It was as if they had summoned her! Malou took one step toward Sara and then noticed Luke seated at the counter. She froze, and her back stiffened. Then she slowly backed up and stopped. Her eyes shifted between Sara and Luke.

"Malou, what's wrong?" Sara regretted the question as soon as it was out of her mouth. The look between Malou and Luke said it all. "I mean, you know, why are you—"

"There's a meeting." Malou held the door open with her foot as if she was ready to bolt. "We all have to see Mrs. Hazelton today. No excuses. Not even your job."

With that, Malou turned and fled. Sara had never seen her look so scared. That stuff that Mrs. Clifford had said about Luke and the fire...Sara couldn't believe that he had had anything to do with that. It was just faulty wiring or old pipes that had caused the disaster. She was absolutely certain of that. But the incident with Malou? That was more disturbing. Mrs. Clifford had even said there was a witness. How could she ignore that?

As the door slammed behind Malou, Luke turned to stare at Sara. "I can't figure you out. You and her," he said, not even calling Malou by her name. "You act like she's your friend."

"Malou is my friend—more like a sister, really!" Sara's anxiety was building, churning her insides into a bubbling cauldron.

"Yeah right!" Luke snickered again. "You want to be friends with a blackie? A Sambo?"

Sara's head throbbed. Should she stand up for Malou? *Yes!* The answer boomed inside of her. And now was her chance to say something. Luke didn't understand her relationship with any of the girls at the orphanage—why she was close to them. It was his one shortcoming. Well, she knew he had more than one, but it was the one that was most obvious. He wanted her all to himself. At least, that's what he always said. She needed to explain all of this to him. So why the hesitation? He loves me, she continued to tell herself. And she knew that she depended on his love, perhaps too much. In the end, she didn't want to mess with that by confronting him. *Coward!*

"Okay, I gotta split." Luke set his coffee cup on the counter and rose from the stool. "I'm gonna see you later, right?"

"What? Oh, no, I can't. I've got to go and see Mrs. Hazelton after work."

"Okay, then after. You can sneak away and come meet me at the garage."

Usually, that offer would have made her heart pound. "I don't know, Luke. It'll probably be late."

Luke gave Sara an icy stare and said, "Tomorrow then. No excuses."

Sara nodded quickly and turned away. She heard the door swing shut behind him. Only then did she release her hands. How long could she go on avoiding the problems that were staring her in the face? Not for long, she thought, as she turned to serve a customer who'd just come in. In the jumble of that confusing interaction with Luke, Sara hadn't even stopped to consider the meeting that Mrs. Hazelton was summoning her to. As she returned to her work, she wondered about her upcoming conversation with the matron.

Four

SARA PASSED WHAT was left of the orphanage on her way to Mrs. Hazelton's cottage after work. She could barely look—it scared her so to see what fire could do to a building. What had once been an imposing two-story mansion was a charred skeleton of its previous glory. The lingering smell of smoke choked her as she bicycled past.

Miraculously, the shed next to the orphanage was still standing, untouched by the fire. It was where Sara and the other six girls would go to talk about private girl things without worrying that Mrs. Hazelton or one of their teachers might barge in on them. It was reassuring for Sara to see that building intact—at least something hadn't been destroyed.

She rested her bike against the wall of Mrs. Hazelton's cottage and walked over the cobblestone steps toward the front door. Her back ached from having slept on the hard wooden pews at the church, and from her long day at the diner, and she stretched her arms overhead and moved her neck from side to side, trying to get the kinks out. Her mind was in free fall, a runaway train of unconnected thoughts. Maybe it was time for her to leave this place anyway and strike out on her own. After all, she was eighteen, a woman, though she didn't really feel like one. Still, other girls her age were married by now—with children. She had proved that she could earn money. Only a couple of the other girls had part-time jobs. And while she didn't really know how much money they made, she was certain that no one had a nest egg like her own.

Sara had rarely thought about leaving the orphanage and had never talked about it with her roommates, except for one conversation she had had with Dot in the common room months ago, and long after the other girls had gone to sleep.

"Really? You'd leave here? I'd be so scared to be on my own!" Dot had said. It was common for Sara and Dot to meet up in the common room after the others had gone to sleep, either poring over the latest style magazines or experimenting with a newfangled stitch or dress pattern. Dot shared Sara's passion for sewing.

Sara had smiled at her roommate. It was no wonder that Mrs. Hazelton referred to Dot as a "young seventeen." She still seemed naïve and uncertain.

"Try a zigzag stitch on the outside, Dot. That's what they're showing in *Seventeen*." The magazine was their bible for clothes, hairstyles and dating advice. Sara walked over to the sewing machine where Dot was laboring over a half-finished blouse—a deep-green muslin number that Sara knew would look fab against Dot's pale skin. "Just think about it. How are we ever going to become famous designers if we stay here?"

"But Miss Webster says we should be happy learning to sew for our future husbands and children," Dot had replied, as if she were reciting an oath. Their home economics teacher was proud of the accomplishments of her two finest sewers, but she never intended for the girls to actually pursue this as a career. She believed that marriage was a woman's highest calling. Teaching and nursing were fine careers for a young girl, Miss Webster reminded them. But dress design? *Maybe for those folks down in Hollywood*, she'd said, wrinkling her nose in disgust. It was a frivolous ambition as far as their teacher was concerned—a hobby more than anything else.

"I've got to dream bigger than that, Dot. And you should too. You're too good at this. I want to go to New York one day, or Paris."

"Paris! That's crazy."

"No, it isn't. Just because we're orphans doesn't mean we can't do something important with our lives."

Sara thought about that conversation as she approached the front door of Mrs. Hazelton's cottage. It had all been innocent talk at the time. Throwing out a destination like Paris was as ridiculous as imagining that men could walk on the moon! Sara had been living in this protected place for so long that it was nearly impossible to imagine another life. But the fire had shaken her deeply. The orphanage was beyond repair—that was clear. So where was she going to go? Another orphanage? That was impossible, given Sara's age and the fact that all orphanages across the province were in the process of closing down. Meeting with Mrs. Hazelton was a good opportunity to talk about her future. But what was that going to be? Something with Luke? That was beginning to seem less and less likely as well.

The transistor radio had been playing softly in the background the night she talked to Dot in the common room, Sara recalled. She and Dot had each doled out some money for the radio, and it provided the perfect rhythm for the sewing needle as it bobbed up and down on the machine. Sometimes they abandoned their sewing completely and just danced to the tunes, doing the Twist and the Mashed Potato. Sara could have cried when she thought about how much she and Dot laughed together as they flew across the floor, hoping Miss Webster or one of the Littles wouldn't hear them. That night, their favorite tune had played in the background, a song called "Runaway." Part of the first verse looped in Sara's mind.

...I wonder
What went wrong
With our love,
A love that was so strong...

Recently Luke had been pressuring her to go all the way. Well, the truth was, he had been pressuring her since the day they started going steady. But lately he had been pushing her more and more to do it, declaring that he loved her—only her—that she was more beautiful than any girl he knew, and that it would be so special to be together that way. And then he would say stuff about guys having "needs" and if he didn't get them met with her, there were plenty of other girls who would be happy to show him a good time.

Sara hated it when he said those things. It wore away at her willpower. And sometimes, though she didn't want to admit it, she suspected that he might be getting his "needs" met with other girls in town. She didn't want to let go of Luke. She had even promised him, if he just waited a little longer, that he would be the one—her first. He seemed to like that and had said he'd wait—not forever, just for a little while. But she knew, deep down, that she didn't want to lose her virginity—not to Luke. For some reason, that didn't feel right, no matter how many times he told her that she was his special girl. And she certainly didn't want to find herself like Vivian Patterson, the girl who had left town mysteriously the previous spring to *visit family in Toronto.*

She left in disgrace, Miss Webster had whispered, almost as a warning to the other girls.

On top of that, Sara was still troubled by the conversation she had had with Luke that morning in the diner. The incident with Malou was not the first antic that he had been involved in. His bad reputation was something that Sara had refused to acknowledge. *Just pranks*, she used to say when Dot criticized Luke. *He's really not a bad guy. Just rough around the edges*. She'd told herself that maybe her roommate was just jealous because she had a boyfriend and Dot didn't. But then there was that rumor that he had been stealing goods from the shelves of the local grocer, Mr. Chin—the only Chinese man who lived in their community. Nothing was ever proved. When Sara had tentatively asked Luke about it, he'd shrugged it off. *Why do you care what happens to him? He shouldn't even be living here—takes away from the decent people of the town.*

The whole thing had left Sara feeling sick. But, again, she'd never pushed it. And that was beginning to make her feel even sicker.

Malou was just leaving Mrs. Hazelton's study when Sara walked into the living room of the cottage. Malou carried a brown manila envelope in her hands, and she had that look in her eyes like she was a million miles away, even though she was standing right in front of Sara.

"Malou? Are you okay?" Sara repeated her name one more time.

"What? Oh, Sara." The two girls hugged tightly before Sara stepped back.

"What's going on? What did you and Mrs. Hazelton talk about?"

Malou shook her head. Sara was beginning to wonder if this had anything to do with Luke. Why else would Malou look like something had just spooked her?

Just then Mrs. Hazelton appeared in the doorway of her office. "Sara. Good, you're here. You're the last of the Seven to meet with me. Come in, please."

Sara looked at Mrs. Hazelton and then stared back at Malou.

"Sara?" Mrs. Hazelton stepped to one side, motioning for Sara to enter her office.

"Yes, ma'am."

But just as Sara was about to walk toward the matron, Malou grabbed her by the arm and leaned over to whisper in her ear. "We all need to say goodbye. Find me, okay? Before you go anywhere." With that, Malou brushed past Sara and left the cottage.

Goodbye? Whatever was Malou talking about?

Mrs. Hazelton cleared her throat, and Sara turned her attention back to the matron. She entered Mrs. Hazelton's office, and the door closed softly behind her as she sank into the large leather chair directly across from the matron's desk. It always startled Sara when she entered Mrs. Hazelton's private sanctuary. It was almost like the feeling she had had seeing her matron in her nightgown—like glimpsing a personal side of Mrs. Hazelton that Sara wasn't really aware of or never thought about. Yes, she knew that Mrs. Hazelton had never married; the girls called her

Mrs. as a show of respect. But beyond that, there was little Sara knew about the matron's life.

Mrs. Hazelton settled heavily into her chair and reached for the half-empty cup of tea, draining it completely before setting it down and leaning forward. It was only then that Sara recalled another piece of personal information she knew about Mrs. Hazelton. Their matron was not well. She had told the girls so a few months earlier, though she hadn't revealed the nature of her ailment.

"How are you, Sara?" Mrs. Hazelton was out of breath. Her face was pale and there were bags under her eyes like two small stuffed pillows. Had the smoke from the previous night's fire aggravated whatever condition she was suffering? Had she lost weight? Why hadn't Sara noticed any of this before?

"Fine, thank you, ma'am. Just trying to get back to normal."

Mrs. Hazelton paused. "Normal...yes, we'd all like to return to the way things were."

"I'm not complaining though. Everyone was really nice to us at the church. I guess we're all just wondering what's going to happen now."

"Yes, there are decisions to be made."

Sara was trying to be patient, but all she could think about was that the orphanage was going to close down and she had no idea what was to become of any of the girls. Malou's final words—*we all need to say goodbye*—rang inside Sara's head. She put her hand on her stomach, as if doing so would quash her growing anxiety. Mrs. Hazelton was speaking again.

"First of all, I want you to know that I have spoken with our board of governors, and we are trying to find homes for each of the younger girls. We have more calls to make, but rest assured, the children will all be taken care of."

That was a relief to Sara. At least the youngest orphans would have temporary homes in other orphanages or, better yet, with real parents and perhaps even siblings. But that still didn't account for the Seven. Sara perched on the edge of her chair, anxious to hear what Mrs. Hazelton was going to say next.

"So that leaves you—my special seven."

It was no secret that Mrs. Hazelton had a soft spot in her heart for the seven oldest girls, those who had been there the longest. She didn't always show it; Mrs. Hazelton took great pains to appear detached and proper. But the girls knew. Sometimes, in those quiet moments when few people were around, she had referred to them this way, as her *special seven,* like a blessed number or a good-luck charm. Sara had never felt particularly lucky.

Two envelopes were sitting on Mrs. Hazelton's desk. The matron nudged the larger manila envelope toward Sara. She looked at the envelope and then back up at Mrs. Hazelton. Malou had been holding a similar envelope when she left the office.

"I'm going to tell you something that you probably already know," Mrs. Hazelton began. "The seven of you—my special seven—will never find homes in families the way the younger ones have."

There it was. Mrs. Hazelton had finally spoken aloud the words that everyone, including Sara, already knew. It was the opportunity that Sara was looking for.

"I've been thinking about that myself, ma'am. I'm glad you asked to talk to all of us—to me. You see—"

"But you mustn't despair about this." Mrs. Hazelton jumped in before Sara could finish her sentence. "You're no longer a child, Sara, and you should have left here when you turned eighteen. I didn't insist on it then, but now, with everything that's happened, it's time for you to make your way out into the world on your own."

Mrs. Hazelton had jumped the gun and said the very words that Sara was about to blurt out.

"I've been keeping some things safe," continued Mrs. Hazelton, "until it was the right time to give them to you and the others. I didn't think it would happen so quickly. But with the fire and all..."

She took a deep breath and pushed the envelope across the desk to Sara. "We've never talked about where you came from and the circumstances of your birth. I think it's time you knew."

Five

THE ENVELOPE SAT in the space between Sara and Mrs. Hazelton until Sara tentatively reached for it. After years of living at the orphanage, she had stopped thinking about the fact that she had come from anywhere. She simply was. Was that the source of her constant anxiety? The fact that she had no history? No roots?

"I don't know everything," Mrs. Hazelton continued as Sara stared down at the envelopes, "but what I do know is all here."

With that, Sara picked up one of the envelopes and turned it over in her hands. Her name, Sara Barry, was written on the front in Mrs. Hazelton's perfect handwriting. With a quick intake of breath, Sara opened the envelope. Three things fell out onto Mrs. Hazelton's desk. The first two looked like documents or certificates. Sara glanced at the first one. It was written in English under a letterhead that said *United Nations Relief and Rehabilitation Administration—UNRRA*. Her gaze shifted to the second document. It looked like a doctor's note, written in a language that she couldn't identify. But it was the third item that drew her attention. It was a thin gold chain, and on the end was suspended a gold star. But this one had six points instead of the usual five. And there was some writing across the front of it in letters that were also unfamiliar to Sara.

"It's a Star of David," said Mrs. Hazelton. "A Jewish star."

Sara nodded. She knew what a Star of David was. Not that she knew anyone who was Jewish, but she had seen pictures of these stars in books. And she had learned a little about the Jewish faith from Reverend Messervey. Mrs. Skelton, their head teacher, once spoke about the Second World War and the Jewish people who had been persecuted in Europe. What did any of this have to do with her?

"I believe it was given to you by your mother," said Mrs. Hazelton gently.

My mother!

Sara knew that she must have had one, of course. But, aside from the fantasy about Coco Chanel, she had stopped thinking about a mother years ago.

Some of the other girls obsessed about their birth mothers and who they might be. Dot had concocted a whole make-believe world about her beginnings. She even wrote letters to herself on the fancy stationery she'd received one Christmas, signed by fantasy mothers like Queen Elizabeth or Sandra Dee! But not Sara. In fact, in some strange way, when she thought about what a mother—her mother—might have looked like, it was Mrs. Hazelton's face that materialized in front of her. That was really the only motherly image she knew. For a moment, Sara's vision went out of focus, and she felt her head begin to swim. She clasped her hands together, beginning to rub them in slow motion, and then stopped, trying to steady herself and breathing deeply. Mrs. Hazelton remained silent, watching Sara as she struggled to compose herself. Finally, Sara picked up the English document and began to read. It was short and to the point.

This female child, born December 20, 1945, in Föhrenwald, Germany, of undetermined nationality, is fit to travel to Canada.

Underneath were two smaller lines. The first one read:

Mother: Karen Frankel

And underneath that:

`Religion: Jewish`

Sara looked up. "Is that her name? My...mother's name?"

"I believe so."

Sara's head was still reeling. "And she was...is... was...Jewish?"

Mrs. Hazelton pointed to the name of the place where Sara had been born. "I'm not sure how it's pronounced—perhaps *Fur-en-vald*, or *For-en-vald*. It was a camp for Jewish refugees who survived the horrors under that monster Adolf Hitler."

Sara nodded. Yes, she knew a little bit—not much—about Adolf Hitler and what he had done to the Jewish people of Europe.

"I believe the second document explains more," added Mrs. Hazelton. "You see, I was told that your mother was imprisoned in a concentration camp and was liberated there at the end of the war." She went on to tell Sara that at some point her mother had contracted TB—tuberculosis—a terrible lung infection that was rampant in the camps. "You were born with the disease, passed on from your mother, after the war ended. You weren't allowed onto the plane when the UNRRA workers wanted to bring you to Canada. Our government was so afraid that citizens here would contract that disease. A friendly doctor in Germany falsified the paperwork, omitting the fact that you had TB. He declared you fit for travel. That's what the second letter says."

Sara glanced once more at the second document. The letters swam in front of her eyes.

"It's written in German," continued Mrs. Hazelton. "This medical certificate is signed by the doctor in Germany. You were treated for the disease here at the orphanage, and you recovered quickly."

Sara looked at the name on the paper—Gunther Pearlman.

She raised her eyes tentatively to Mrs. Hazelton. "And my...father?" The word sounded like another language in her mouth.

Mrs. Hazelton shook her head. "I assume he was imprisoned with your mother. But I'm afraid I have no information about him."

Sara sat back in her chair. She was still having difficultly processing it all—the fire, realizing that she was no longer going to be able to live at the orphanage, and now hearing that her mother was Jewish and connected to the horrible events of the Second World War.

Mrs. Hazelton rose and moved around her desk. She paused in front of Sara and then eased herself into another chair, wincing, as if the effort of holding herself up was suddenly too much. Once again, Sara remembered that the matron was ill. It was so selfish of her to think only of herself in that moment. "What about you, ma'am? Are you in pain?"

Mrs. Hazelton brushed the question away. "We cannot always control what becomes of our bodies, my dear. But it will give me peace of mind to know that the seven of you are making your way in the world." She paused. "And there's one more thing."

More?

It was then that Mrs. Hazelton reached for a second envelope, still on the desk. "I want to help you in any way I can," she said. "Since I discovered some time ago that the orphanage would be closing, I've been saving what little money I could, putting it away until the day that I could give it to you—to each one of my special seven. This is yours."

She handed the second envelope to Sara, who opened it carefully and extracted a handful of worn bills.

"There is $138 there. It could have been more if the fire hadn't happened, and I'd had more time. But it will help get you started. I know you've also been accumulating money from your job." Mrs. Hazelton smiled at Sara's astonished look. "Of course I know about your savings. Where would you have possibly spent the money you've been earning at Loretta's?"

"But what am I supposed to do with all of this?" It was all too much for Sara to grasp.

Mrs. Hazelton stared intently at Sara before replying. "I can tell some of the others where they must go, but not you, Sara. Not any longer. I can give you information, help you think about your options. But I can no longer make decisions for you. This may be difficult for you to hear, but you're going to have to figure some of this out on your own. You have a couple more days to decide."

"I still don't quite understand, ma'am. Are you telling me I need to leave? Right away?" All of Sara's big thinking about moving on had evaporated. She wanted nothing more than to stay where life was familiar and safe.

"Yes, that's what I'm telling you." Mrs. Hazelton's gaze was penetrating.

"And you're not going to tell me where...or how?"

Mrs. Hazelton paused and then reached over to take Sara's hand. "You need to get on with your life, dear. There simply is no alternative. But here's my advice to you. Sometimes I think it's important to look back in order to move forward. Find out where you came from, and in so doing, take a step forward in your own life—independently, strongly, with conviction, and knowing who you are. That's all I'm going to say."

"How am I supposed to do that?" Sara's anxiety was mounting by the second. And Mrs. Hazelton was giving her riddles instead of answers.

"Think about what I've told you today, Sara. You can remain at the church for a couple more days until you think through what you are going to do." With that, Mrs. Hazelton rose and moved over to open the door, indicating that their meeting was over.

Sara left the office more shaken than ever. Mrs. Hazelton had left her with more questions than answers, and she needed time to process everything—but time was slipping away. What was it the matron had said? *Sometimes you need to look back in order to move forward.* Sara was never one for looking back. But it appeared that she might have to start.

Six

THE NEXT DAY, as soon as her shift was over at Loretta's, Sara headed for the town library to do some research. It had been difficult for her to get through her day. She had been so distracted by her previous evening's conversation with Mrs. Hazelton that she was quite a mess during her shift, mixing up orders, dropping a ketchup bottle on the floor and spilling several cups of coffee, one of them on Reverend Messervey, who left the restaurant soaking wet. Sara was mopping up the mess when Mrs. Clifford, patient as ever, finally jumped in to question her.

"I know you haven't been sleeping much, but are you sure you haven't been drinking?" she asked, leaning forward as if she was trying to smell Sara's breath. "Were you out partying with that boyfriend of yours?" Sara never drank, though it was common knowledge that Luke sometimes had one too many. "How many times do I have to warn you—"

"I'm so sorry, Mrs. Clifford," Sara interrupted, before her boss could jump on Luke. "I don't know what's gotten into me. Just a little tired, I guess, what with the fire and sleeping at the church and all, and not really knowing what's going to happen."

That seemed to satisfy Mrs. Clifford, who backed off. "I know you've got a lot on your mind right now. But please try and focus, dear. I can't have you spilling coffee on the customers, especially the reverend! It's bad for business."

"Yes, ma'am." It had taken all of Sara's determination to finish off the day without any more mishaps.

The town library was housed in a small clapboard building behind the church. It contained a modest collection of books and reference material, managed by the same church ladies who had organized Sara and the other orphans after the fire. It was an unwritten rule around town that if someone died, their books would be donated here. The collection of reading material that had been amassed over the years was as strangely eclectic as the citizens of Hope, ranging from mysteries to books on farm equipment. Sara parked her bicycle next to the building. Mrs. Riley was sitting behind the small desk at the entrance, and she looked up as Sara entered. Her daughter, Christine, had once worked at Loretta's but lost her job when Mrs. Clifford caught her with her hand in the till. The town had buzzed about it for weeks, and it was months before Christine could show her face. Sara had always felt a bit sorry for her—never believed she was a bad person. And in a strange way, it was Christine who was responsible for Sara being hired at Loretta's. Mrs. Clifford had offered her the job a couple of days after Christine's abrupt dismissal.

Sara smiled briefly at Mrs. Riley before heading for the *World Book Encyclopedia* to look up information on the Holocaust. She stared at a picture of Adolf Hitler, a little man with beady eyes and cropped bristles for a mustache. She needed to understand the history, especially the number of Jewish people who had perished under his tyranny, along with how they were killed in the concentration camps. The statistics took Sara's breath away—millions murdered by cruel methods of torture. Who could believe such things were possible? At times, Sara had to close her eyes to the hideous photographs of mass graves and skeletal corpses. She couldn't begin to imagine the evil that had led to this outcome. And somehow, her own mother had been a victim of it all. That was even harder to imagine.

But she had work to do. So she tried to push the grisly pictures to the back of her mind. She needed to find something about Föhrenwald, the place that one of her documents said she had been born. That information was harder to find. There wasn't much in the encyclopedia about it, except to say that it had been one of the displaced persons (DP) camps that were established after the war for Jews who had survived but were sick and had nowhere to go. This one had closed in 1957. There had been several barracks to house the Jewish refugees, and even a school. When she tried to find Föhrenwald on a map of Germany, the closest big city appeared to be Munich. Sara stared at the dot on the map. What do I do with all of this, she wondered. Is that where I'm supposed to be going? Is that where I'm going to find out about my mother and my life? All the clues to Sara's identity were pointing her in the direction of Germany. But the idea of traveling there was overwhelming. Why was Mrs. Hazelton being so vague about what Sara was supposed to do? "Just tell me the answer," she whispered.

The last thing Sara did before leaving the building was to take out a copy of *The Diary of Anne Frank*, wondering briefly who had left the book to the library. She intended to read it when everyone was asleep. Mrs. Riley glanced curiously at Sara as she stamped the book. "That's quite an interesting choice you've made," she said.

Sara nodded but didn't respond. She wasn't ready to talk to anyone about this, not before she had had a chance to talk to Luke. She found him at the garage, working on a pickup truck.

"Hey, I missed you last night," he said, raising his head briefly before disappearing under the hood.

Sara felt her heart skip a beat, as it usually did when she was close to Luke. But this time her longing was mixed with something else. Was it fear? What was he going to think—and say—when she told him what she had discovered about her mother and herself? She closed her eyes and took a deep breath, waiting impatiently for him to finish his work. A full half hour passed before Luke finally closed the hood of the truck and reached for a dirty rag to wipe the black grease from his hands. By then, Sara could barely contain herself. She blurted her news and then stood back to watch Luke's reaction.

At first he smiled, as if she had just told him a funny story. But the smile quickly faded from his face. "What do you mean, you were born in Germany?" he asked, throwing the dirty rag off to one side and reaching for a bottle of soda that was open and sitting on the workbench. At least this time he hadn't grabbed a cigarette. His overalls were smeared with the same grease as his hands were. The overalls looked as if they had never been washed. Luke always said that he liked it that way, that it made it seem like he was really working hard at his job. "I never figured you were some kind of Kraut," he added, taking a long swig of his drink.

Sara ignored the comment, though she knew the term was offensive. There was more to tell. She reached inside her blouse and extracted the necklace with the Star of David. She had put it on after leaving Mrs. Hazelton's cottage and had worn it ever since, though it was inside her blouse and not visible for anyone to see—until now.

Luke stared at the star. "What the hell is that?"

"It's a Jewish star." Sara took another deep breath. A strange sense of calm had descended on her—an unfamiliar feeling. She stared evenly at her boyfriend. "Mrs. Hazelton told me I am Jewish."

Sara had never seen Luke at a loss for words. He scratched at the back of his neck and rubbed his jaw, shaking his head from side to side. He avoided her stare. After a full minute of scratching and fumbling, he collected himself and looked Sara in the eye. "You're a Kraut and a Jew? How's that even possible? I thought all you people were burned up back in the war."

It was Sara's turn to be taken aback. A slow burn was igniting in the pit of her stomach. All those times that Dot and Malou and Mrs. Clifford and others had cautioned her about Luke suddenly flashed through her mind. All those times she had chosen to ignore their warnings about how he treated people, even when it was all there in front of her eyes. She was confused by the insensitivity of his comment. But most of all, she was angry. She wrapped her arms around her body to keep from shaking.

"Do you have any idea what you're talking about, Luke?" Her voice was controlled but steely enough for him to know she was dead serious. "Do you realize how cruel and stupid that comment is?" Did she really just call him stupid? It appeared there was no stopping her now. "Do you even know how many Jewish people were killed then—or how?" It was the first time Sara could remember confronting her boyfriend—or anyone, for that matter. She wasn't even sure what it was that she was standing up for. It wasn't as if she felt Jewish or connected to that religion—or to any religion. She was still trying to figure out what all of that meant for her. But Luke's ignorance had pushed her to the edge. For the first time that she could remember, she was standing up for something, and it felt good.

Luke's face went from white to a deep shade of red. "Hey, come on. Don't flip your wig. What are you getting all peeved about?"

Sara clutched her body even tighter. Her face prickled with heat. "I can't believe you can even ask me that question. Millions, Luke. That's how many Jewish people died. Millions!"

Luke stepped forward and tried to take Sara in his arms. "Come on, baby. I don't want to fight. I've got better things to do with my time."

Sara pushed him away and tossed her dark curls over her shoulder. "So have I! I'm going to Germany." There! She had said it. It was all so obvious—had been from the moment Mrs. Hazelton gave her the envelopes. She had just needed time to put it together. And here it was, all the pieces lining up in a row just like the chessmen on the set that Joe kept in his room. Joe would have said it was as plain as the nose on her face. Telling Luke that she was going to Germany felt right. And in putting those words out there, Sara realized that she was already taking the first step of her journey.

Luke laughed. "Sure, baby. And I'm going to Mars."

He tried to reach for her again, but Sara turned and walked out the door of the garage. It was amazing to her that she felt so strong, so energized. "Keep walking," she whispered to herself, knowing that every step away from Luke would be a step toward independence. Perhaps she'd cry over him later. But not now. Now she had to move forward and keep her head together. There was so much to do if she was really going to head for Germany, she realized, so much to think about and plan. But first, she had to say goodbye to the people who really counted.

Seven

SHE STARTED WITH Mrs. Clifford, thinking that would be the easiest goodbye. She was wrong. Sara's boss was unusually weepy.

"I just can't imagine what I'm going to do around here without you," Mrs. Clifford said, dabbing at her eyes with her apron. "I've come to rely on you for everything. You've been one of the best waitresses I've ever had."

Sara tried not to smile. "You didn't think that all those times I was mixing up orders, ma'am."

"None of that matters now. You're a smart girl, Sara. I knew that the minute I met you. And you're a fast learner. I just can't believe you're going to be leaving."

"I want to thank you for giving me this job, Mrs. Clifford. You have no idea how helpful it's been."

That was true, though Mrs. Clifford might not have guessed that it was the salary that had been most helpful, especially now that Sara was planning her trip to Germany. She hadn't shared too much information about that with her boss except to say that, in the aftermath of the fire, it was time to do something with her life and to move on to another place. "All the girls are going to be leaving," she added.

"It'll be good for you to start fresh in some other city," Mrs. Clifford said. "Find a nice young man for yourself, Sara. Not that thug you've been hanging out with."

Sara bent to hug Mrs. Clifford, ignoring the last comment.

"You're a good girl, Sara. I just don't know what I'm going to do here without you." Mrs. Clifford was getting tearful again and starting to repeat herself.

"You'll have no trouble finding someone else to take my place here, ma'am. Girls will be lining up for this job."

She hadn't expected her boss to be so emotional. And for a moment, Sara found herself unsettled by the sudden knowledge that she would be missed. As an orphan, she had always felt like one of the undesirables in this town, except for the attention Luke paid her, and that came with all kinds of other problems. But she was taken aback to discover that

Mrs. Clifford cared so much about her. It made their goodbye so much more heartbreaking. But Sara also knew that saying goodbye to Mrs. Clifford was a piece of cake compared to saying goodbye to the other Seven.

She caught up with Malou in the shed on the orphanage property. It seemed that for now, Malou was more comfortable staying there than at the church. But Sara knew it would probably not be for long. Once Malou figured things out, she told Sara, she would be heading for northern Ontario to follow the clues that Mrs. Hazelton had given her.

"I'm sorry," Sara said, after she and Malou had hugged and caught up on their respective plans.

"For what?"

"For not standing up for you—all those times that Luke came after you, badgered you. I knew about them. I should have said something and I never did. I'm sorry."

Malou looked away.

Every second that passed felt like an eternity to Sara. "I know that doesn't fix everything," she finally said, trying to fill the empty air.

"It helps. Thank you."

Sara felt tears well up in her eyes. "I'm going to Germany. Can you imagine that?"

Malou's eyes widened. "It's so far away."

"I know." Sara reached into her blouse and pulled out the Star of David. "It has something to do with this. Mrs. Hazelton told me that my mother was Jewish. That means I am as well."

Malou stared at the star and then up at Sara. "It kind of makes you different from everyone too."

Sara felt another weight lift off her shoulders. It wasn't as if she suddenly understood how Malou had really felt being the only colored girl in the orphanage. All Sara knew was that the discovery that she was Jewish by birth had touched something in her. She had always felt different just because she was an orphan. But that was something she shared with all of the girls. How much more different had Malou felt all these years?

"I'm not sure when we'll see each other again," Sara continued. "But maybe I'll write to you. Mrs. Clifford says that she'll pass on any letters, if we send them to the diner, once she knows where we've ended up."

Malou nodded. "What about your boyfriend?"

Sara sighed. "I'm happy to be leaving him behind."

Tracking down the others proved more difficult than Sara had thought. The seven girls were scattering in seven directions, and most of the others had already left. Tess was gone, though that didn't surprise Sara. So was Cady, who had left a note behind saying that she was heading for Toronto. She had no firm plans other than to find a place to stay and a job. Cady's note said nothing about who she would be searching for or what Mrs. Hazelton had given her in the way of information.

It was Dot who filled Sara in on what had become of all the girls. She met up with Dot one last time back at the church. After the night of the fire, Dot had moved in with the Welshes, who were only too happy to have her there since their own daughter, Lorraine, was away for the summer. Dot was all decked out in a print dress that Mrs. Welsh had given her.

"It's Lorraine's," Dot said, smoothing down the skirt. "Mrs. Welsh has been really nice to me. She's given me a bunch of her daughter's things. Nicest clothes I ever had," she added.

Sara nodded. She and Dot had dreamed of a wardrobe like Lorraine's. Funny how this handout had come to Dot by way of the fire—just another example of some good coming out of the tragedy, she guessed. The girls were sitting in the pews, just the two of them. In the preceding couple of days, all the Little Ones had been farmed out, some to families, and some to temporary homes until more permanent placements could be found. The chapel seemed more cavernous than ever.

"Toni took off as soon as she had her meeting with Mrs. H.," Dot said once they got down to talking about the Seven. "She headed straight for the road to catch a bus to Toronto. But Joe must have guessed that she was going to leave. He found her waiting by the side of the road and drove her to the bus stop in town."

"Do you know what she's going to do in Toronto?"

Dot shook her head. "That's all I know. Joe might know more, but he isn't saying much—keeping it all pretty close to the chest. You know Joe. He'd take a secret to his grave." She paused. "Toni didn't wait to say goodbye to any of us."

"I know. I expected that of Tess, but not Toni. Do you think she said goodbye to Betty?"

"I'm sure she must have. Those two wouldn't do anything without talking to the other."

For a moment, the two girls retreated into silence. Dot had also told Sara that Betty had left the same day as Toni, bound for Kingston. Once again, there was no other information about what she was seeking. Even Dot herself was being quiet about her upcoming journey. She had returned to the church with an envelope similar to Sara's, probably the one containing the $138 from Mrs. Hazelton, Sara guessed. But Dot also carried a man's large double-breasted overcoat. Did that have something to do with her past? Sara didn't ask and Dot didn't offer up any information. That suited Sara fine. She was still trying to process everything that Mrs. Hazelton had told her. And apart from telling Dot about her upcoming trip, Sara wasn't ready to talk too much about it. It was simply enough to know that the girls were going in separate directions, each one bound up in a personal journey.

"Looks like we're going to be traveling after all." Sara was the one to break the silence. She reminded Dot about their late-night conversation in the common room before the fire. "Do you remember when I said that I wanted to see New York or Paris?"

"And now you're going to Germany! Now *that's* a real trip. I'm just going to another small town." Dot was heading north to a place called Buckminster. That much, Sara knew.

"You and I will get to Paris one day, Dot. I'm sure of it!"

"I don't know," Dot replied, blinking back tears. "I never thought I'd leave this place."

"I don't think many of us did. But let's make a pact—you and me. We're going to be famous dress designers one day." Sara sat up in her pew, suddenly animated. "That'll show Miss Webster and everyone back here in Hope. I know we can do it."

Dot swallowed hard, unable to talk.

"And we'll meet back here. One year from now. Let's say, June 6." The anniversary of the fire. Dot nodded and reached across the pew to grab Sara's hand and squeeze it hard. That sealed the deal as far as Sara was concerned.

~

And that left Mrs. Hazelton. It was the goodbye that Sara was dreading most. But tracking the matron down was almost as difficult as finding her roommates. Immediately after meeting with the Seven, Mrs. Hazelton had left her cottage and moved to a quiet nursing home in Cartwright, a town about ten miles east of Hope. At first, Sara thought that might be it; she would never see the matron again. That thought had filled her with such despair. That's when Mrs. Clifford had stepped in, magically appearing at the church as if she had had a premonition that Sara needed her help. She offered to drive Sara over to visit with Mrs. Hazelton, and Sara had not hesitated in taking her up on it. Sara found the matron sitting in a rocking chair on the porch of the nursing home, wrapped in a light shawl and reading a book.

"Joe brought me here," Mrs. Hazelton explained. "He's a good man." She paused before continuing.

"I don't know how long I'll need to be here, Sara. But I just knew I couldn't stay at the cottage on my own any longer." Mrs. Hazelton sighed and looked off into the distance. "My bad health was catching up with me, quicker than I had thought it would."

Sara sensed how painful this admission was. Indeed, the matron was looking worse. Even though only a couple of days had passed since their last visit, Sara noticed that she seemed to have grown paler and had somehow shrunk before Sara's eyes. The realization that Mrs. Hazelton needed help looking after herself was another blow. How sick was she? And with what? Did she have anyone in her life who would be able to care for her? Where would she go after the nursing home? Sara longed to ask these questions but knew it wasn't her place.

"But I'm so glad you've come." Mrs. Hazelton sat forward in her rocking chair and pulled the shawl tighter around her shoulders. "I had hoped you would visit."

"I'm going to Germany," Sara blurted out.

Mrs. Hazelton smiled as if this came as no surprise to her.

"Mrs. Clifford helped me find a travel agent to book my ticket." Sara had had no idea how to make the flight arrangements, and after finally confessing the details of her trip to her boss, Mrs. Clifford had been only too happy to help.

"Mrs. Clifford is a good person," Mrs. Hazelton replied. "I know how much she cares for you."

The silence that followed echoed loudly in the still air.

"What if I can't do this?" Sara finally said. She realized that she had no idea what she was doing. Up until that moment, she had existed in a small square of a town. Now, it was as if she had been shoved off the map of her life.

Mrs. Hazelton's voice was calm. "There is no failure here, Sara, just discovery."

"What if I need to get in touch with you? Can I call you?" She didn't want to sound needy, especially when Mrs. Hazelton was dealing with her own ill health. But Sara could feel the panic twisting her up inside. She couldn't control it any longer, couldn't pretend that everything was fine. Her hands began to twist together, rubbing against one another in a slow circular motion.

"You won't need me," Mrs. Hazelton replied gently but firmly, leaning forward and pulling Sara's hands apart. Her face was inches from Sara's. "I've raised you to be independent and to rely on yourself—you and all my girls."

"But what if I'm in trouble?" Sara had been cool and composed for long enough. This goodbye was taking her over the edge, crushing the air out of her lungs. She tried to take a deep breath, but it was no good. What was she thinking, running off to Germany of all places? She didn't feel independent or self-reliant, as Mrs. Hazelton was suggesting. She was simply scared.

Mrs. Hazelton was talking again, her voice a soothing metronome bringing Sara back into her body and helping her breathe once more. "You know you can always write. And Mrs. Clifford will pass your letters on to me." Sara nodded, not trusting herself to speak.

"And Sara, there's one more thing. You're a quiet girl, but I know you have a spirit that is fierce. Find a way to draw on that as you go forward. Don't be led by that apprehension that burns deep inside of you. You may have been able to hide it from others, but not from me. It will help if you figure out where that comes from."

Sara swallowed hard. "I'll try, ma'am." No one knew her as well as Mrs. Hazelton did. At least the matron was not giving her a lecture about Luke. She wouldn't have been able to deal with that.

"This journey will be so good for you, Sara," added Mrs. Hazelton. "Just remember what I told you about the importance of looking back. That will keep you going. I'm certain of it."

Mrs. Hazelton reached over to hug Sara, who collapsed in her arms. "I'll never forget you." Sara's voice was muffled against Mrs. Hazelton's shoulder.

A quaver arose in the matron's reply. "Nor I you."

Eight

THE PLANE JOLTED and shook. Sara clutched the arms of her seat, her knuckles white and bulging. The captain had warned of a bumpy ride, but Sara hadn't really known what to expect. She tightened her seat belt across her waist, lifted the blind from the window and gazed out at the mountain of clouds below. How does this massive piece of metal stay up in the air, she wondered, glancing over at the elderly man seated next to her. Just before takeoff he had crossed himself, twice! That had unnerved her as well. But now he was fast asleep—head back, mouth open, snoring loudly. His eyeglasses were perched on the tip of his nose, threatening to fall off if he moved an inch. Sara needed to get to the bathroom, but she wasn't sure how to get past him without waking him up.

This was all so new to her—the flight, the turbulence, the confined seating. It was the first time she had ever flown—at least, as far back as she could remember. Maybe there had been a plane ride once before, years earlier, that had brought her to Canada and to the orphanage. But it was erased from her memory, as if it had never existed. She hadn't slept on this flight and hadn't eaten a thing. Her stomach was churning. She had to get to the bathroom!

The flight was bound for Munich, the city in the southern part of Germany that was closest to Föhrenwald, the DP camp. Once she landed in Munich, she would take a train southwest to the town of Wolfratshausen. Another strange name. Sara had taken to breaking down these difficult names, sounding them out and trying to simplify them. Wolf-rats-house-en. Not very appealing, she thought. The name made it sound as bad as Hope, only harder to pronounce! But it was also the last known address for Gunther Pearlman, the doctor who had signed the medical certificate that Mrs. Hazelton had given her. Wolfratshausen was therefore her destination. With Mrs. Clifford's help, she had booked a return flight to Toronto in seven days. Not too much time to discover everything about where I came from, she thought wryly. But she figured it would have to be enough. Plus, that was about as far as her nest egg would take her—flights, somewhere to stay, food. Seven days had to do it.

In the bus, on the way to the airport, Sara had passed the sign on the other side of town.

You are now leaving Hope

Leaving Hope. She couldn't help but smile at that ironic declaration. Was she really leaving hope behind, or was she going to discover it halfway around the world?

All *this* was new to her too—being on her own and having to make decisions about where she was going to stay and what she was going to eat. Most of those decisions had been made for her all her life—for her and the other six. At the thought of the Seven, Sara gripped her seat arms even tighter and leaned her head back against the headrest. She couldn't think about the others too much; she would start to cry if she let her mind go there. But she couldn't help wondering, if only for a moment, where her roommates were. She had tried to pry more information from Joe when she bumped into him after leaving Mrs. Hazelton's nursing home. But, just as she thought, Joe was being quiet about the journeys of the other girls.

"Now Sara," he had said, scratching at his chin and squinting at her, "I'm not about to tell any secrets.

Joe knows when to keep his mouth shut. If the other girls want you to know where they're goin', they'll likely get in touch with you themselves." It was then that she had told him about her upcoming trip to Germany. Joe nodded as if he'd known this all along. "Sounds like you got enough on your plate without worrying about the others."

"Have you ever been to Europe, Joe?" Sara asked.

"Europe?" Joe smiled as he peered at her, then laughed that deep, rumbling laugh of his. Sara was going to miss that. "Nah. I've traveled a bit around here but never anywhere that far. But I guess it's going to be time for me to move on too."

With the devastation at the orphanage, Joe had also lost his home. He had told Sara that he was going to be moving to Toronto.

"I'm stayin' here in Cartwright for now. Just makin' sure that Miz Hazelton is going to be okay. And then I'll be gone." He paused. "We're all going exploring. Yup. That's the truth, Sara. Some close, some far. You don't have to go too far to be on a journey. That's the truth too."

Sara stared back at Joe. Even with little or no education, he was possibly one of the wisest men she knew. "I just want to know that everyone's going to be okay."

"You girls are all going to be fine. Miz Hazelton raised you right."

And that was that. A quick hug and Joe had disappeared.

~

The man next to Sara inhaled sharply and coughed, sputtering and lurching forward in his seat. His eyes sprang open, and his glasses went flying. Sara gulped down a laugh and seized the opportunity. "Excuse me," she said, pointing down the aisle toward the bathrooms. The man was groping around for his eyeglasses. Sara spotted them on the floor and bent forward to pick them up.

"Ah, tenk you," he said in heavily accented English. "Toilet?" She nodded.

In the bathroom, Sara ran cold water across her palms. She had ground her hands so hard in the takeoff that she had rubbed some skin away from one of her fingers. The blister was raw and sore, and the cool water helped to ease the burn. Then she splashed some water on her face and stared at herself in the mirror. Her hair was a curly mess, and she pulled it back into a tight ponytail to get it off her face. Her blue eyes stared back at her as she wondered for the millionth time what she would find in Germany. She had the name of the doctor and an address. She didn't have much else, except for the Star of David necklace, which was still around her neck but now more prominently displayed on the outside of her blouse. She toyed with it absently as she gazed at her reflection.

Sara had had one last conversation with Luke before she left town. She hadn't meant to talk to him. She had figured it was over and it was best to leave it at that. But Luke had ambled into Loretta's when Sara was there picking up an old suitcase that Mrs. Clifford had given her for the trip. They practically ran headlong into each other, and the sudden closeness sent shivers running up and down Sara's spine. What is that? she asked herself. Anger? Nerves? Desire? What? In the last twenty-four hours, her resolve to leave him had wavered. Not a lot—just enough to upset her. Would she ever find anyone to love her? she wondered. Would she end up like Miss Webster, whom everyone called a spinster? Their teacher had never seemed very happy. Sara had even started wondering if Mrs. Hazelton had ever regretted not getting married.

"What are you doing here?" she blurted out. He was a bit puffy-faced and his eyes were tired, like he hadn't been sleeping much.

Luke nodded toward the counter. "Coffee."

Of course. I'm a ditz, she thought. Luke hadn't come looking for her. Besides, why did she even care why he was there?

"You planning on leaving soon?" Luke indicated the suitcase.

"Umm, yes. Tomorrow, actually." Sara placed the suitcase on the floor and rested her hand on her belly to stop the acrobatics that were going on inside of her.

Luke shuffled one foot in front of him, like he was trying to kick at some imaginary dust on the floor. "You know, I've been thinking," he said. "I'm glad I ran into you here. You and me, we kind of got off on the wrong foot the other day. I didn't want to fight with you, Sara. And I know you didn't want to fight with me." He reached out and rubbed the top of her arm lightly with the back of his fingers.

Sara inhaled sharply, and for just a moment she yearned for Luke's hand to stay there. But then she quickly shrugged him off. Where was this going? Was Luke going to apologize to her? That would be a first!

"So..." He shuffled a bit more and then looked up. "Look, I don't care if you're a Jew or a Kraut or anything else. What are people going to think with you taking off like this? You should just forget this stupid trip and stay here with me."

Sara stiffened. "What?"

"You heard me. I'm telling you to stay with me." There was a long pause. Luke looked away and then back at Sara. And then he lowered his voice and added, "Please."

For a split second Sara thought she was going to faint right there on the floor. Was Luke really asking her to stay? Begging her? Just like the way she used to beg him to call or to show up at the diner. It was like they had suddenly switched places.

He stood in front of her, waiting, a bit hound-like, shuffling and fidgeting. And in that moment, all of Sara's torment and uncertainty melted away. Of course she had made the right decision in saying goodbye to him, and she was also certain that he would never understand that. He would never fully appreciate her or what she was embarking on. She was a conquest to him, and it had pricked his ego to be losing her. That much she was sure of. Strangely, she didn't feel angry with him or even anxious, the way she usually did. She felt kind of sorry for him. It was a new feeling. His life was so narrow, and she realized how little he understood of people. When had she become so worldly?

"Come on, baby." Luke leaned toward her. "Say something. People are staring at us."

Sara looked around the diner. Sure enough, several of the customers had stopped eating. Forks and spoons hovered in midair. Dr. Blunt and his wife were at a table in one corner, and Reverend Messervey was seated at a booth across from them. Mrs. Riley was there, along with a couple of the other ladies from the church. They all had their eyes glued to the scene at the front of the diner, listening and waiting to see what was going to happen. Sara returned their gazes, evenly and assuredly. She turned to face Luke one last time. Then she picked up the suitcase. Silently, chin high in the air, she pushed past him and walked out of Loretta's.

"*Verehrte Damen und Herren*—ladies and gentlemen, please return to your seats and fasten your seat belts as we begin our descent into Munich. We will be landing shortly."

Sara was jolted out of her memories. Underneath her feet, the plane dipped and listed to the right. She rested the Star of David back on her chest and patted it lightly. It was time.

Nine

AND HERE SHE was, all alone and in a foreign country. Sara descended from the train at Wolfratshausen station after having taken the Isar Valley Railway from Munich, a forty-kilometer ride aboard the electric train. She was exhausted after the long trip from Canada. How long had it been since she had slept? Or eaten? Her head was spinning. Thank goodness the train ride had been smooth, not like the roller-coaster plane trip, which still had her gut twisted up in knots.

She fingered the Star of David around her neck. She had tucked it back inside her blouse after an uncomfortable encounter with the German customs officer at the airport. He had stared openly at it when he asked the purpose of her visit to Germany.

"I've come to visit my family," Sara replied. It wasn't a complete lie. After all, she was coming to find out about her mother, father and anyone else who had been part of her life. There wasn't much else she could say without arousing too much curiosity. *I'm an orphan. I've lost my home and suddenly discovered that my mother, whom I never knew, is Jewish and was in a concentration camp*. That would have led to all kinds of other impossible questions. A short answer was best, Sara thought, even if it was a bit vague. Joe would have said, *A little white lie is what I call a harmless untruth.*

"And how long will you be here...visiting your family?" the customs official asked.

"Just a week." Sara tried to keep her voice light. That was when she half-expected him to ask, *Are you Jewish? And what is a Jewish girl doing here in Germany?* She didn't know why she anticipated a sharp interrogation. It was just that the look on his face was far from inviting. Fortunately, he didn't say another word, just waved her through. After that, she had concealed the star back inside her blouse. Maybe that was just the way it was going to be for a while, until she figured things out. Her life, like the necklace, would sometimes be hidden away and sometimes out there for all to see.

Finding the train had been another adventure. Sara had managed to make her way to the Munich train station, even managed to buy a ticket to Wolfratshausen. Thank goodness the woman at the ticket office had spoken English. Waiting on the train track, holding the ticket in her hand, Sara had approached an elderly man.

"Excuse me, is this the platform for the train to Wolfratshausen?" It was becoming easier and easier to pronounce the name of the town.

The man smiled, revealing black spaces where teeth used to be. Then he bowed slightly and tipped his fedora. He was about to move on without responding when Sara stopped him once more.

"I'm looking for platform three." Why was she raising her voice, as if that would somehow enable him to understand what she was saying? She held up three fingers. "Platform three," she repeated.

"*Ja, ja*," the man replied, nodding and pointing toward the tracks right in front of her. "*Drei*."

Drei. It must mean three. "I think the train is late..." Sara began again in a more even tone, but by then the man had moved off, but not before bowing deeply and tipping his hat once more.

Eventually, the train had arrived and she'd boarded, hugging her suitcase to her knees. As the train moved off, Sara felt herself relax for the first time since leaving the airplane. Outside the window the countryside zoomed by: small farmhouses surrounded by wooden fences and densely packed forests. In the distance white-capped mountains loomed over the landscape. It was hot inside the train, and packed. Every seat was taken, and the less fortunate overflow crowd stood in the center of the aisle, jammed against one another, holding on to seat backs and overhead bars and swaying back and forth as one mass. Sara was lucky to have claimed a seat in one corner. A little blond girl sitting in front of her turned around to stare. She was all decked out in a plaid overcoat and matching hat, an outfit that Sara or Dot could have easily made if they had the material and a machine. Sara smiled and extended her hand. But just as the little girl was about to grasp it, the woman sitting next to her muttered something in German, and the girl twisted around in her seat and plopped back down. Sara's head began to bob forward onto her chest. Sleep! She longed for it. Perhaps for just a few minutes...A whistle blew, and Sara jerked back up in her seat. What was she thinking? She couldn't nap! What if she missed her stop? There would be no way to ask for directions if she got lost. No matter what, she had to force herself to stay awake. Fortunately, the trip was relatively short, and before she knew it, the porter announced their arrival at Wolfratshausen station.

And here she was.

It was hot, warmer than she had expected it to be on this June morning. The sun beat down on Sara as she stood alone on the platform. She closed her eyes and turned her face up to the bright light, letting the rays wash over her. Just then an old woman rode by on a rusty bicycle. The creaking wheels announced her arrival even before the bicycle itself appeared. Sara brought her face away from the sun and gazed in the direction of the rider. The woman was ancient—as least as far as Sara was concerned. She wore a black scarf tied tightly under her chin, a black sweater buttoned to her neck and a black skirt that rode up as she pedaled by to reveal black stockings and sturdy black shoes. The woman was shrouded in black.

Sara giggled in spite of herself. "Where have I landed?" she said aloud to no one. "And what am I doing here?" Suddenly, the absurdity of it all came crashing down on her, along with Mrs. Hazelton's instructions on the necessity of looking back. Why was that so important? Sara asked herself for the millionth time. She had lived her eighteen years with hardly a glance at her past. And she had done fine, thank you very much! Well, perhaps not fine, but okay. And okay was better than nothing and better than many people did. All of a sudden, she was learning that she came from a different religion and had a connection to a dark time in history. Why was that worth knowing about? And how was that going to help her move forward in her life with her dream of dress design, or finding a husband who would treat her well and who could be a true partner?

Just before leaving Hope to travel to Germany, Sara had finally read *The Diary of Anne Frank*, the book she had borrowed from the town library. Well, the truth was, she had actually devoured it, absorbing the entire book in one sitting. It was mesmerizing—the words of a young girl who had been forced to give up her freedom and hide away. At the last minute Sara had decided not to return the book to the library. Instead, she had tucked it into her suitcase. No one was going to miss it, she reasoned. Besides, she had felt a strange connection to Anne, was moved by the innocence of her young life. Anne loved a boy her own age, dreamed of being a journalist, longed for friends and thought about growing up...all the things that normal young people did. *All the things that I do*. The big difference was that the backdrop for Anne's life was a war that had killed millions of people. If Anne had survived, would she have wanted to look back? Sara wondered. Not that she was comparing her life with Anne's. That was undeserved! Nothing could compare with that tragedy. But she was still wondering if looking back was really the answer.

Sara sighed loudly. There was no one to hear her in the deserted train station. The old woman dressed in black had long disappeared, riding over a small ridge leading into what looked like the town. There was a small white building behind Sara, but when she entered to get directions, the man behind the counter spoke no English.

"Excuse me," she began. "I need to get into town and find this address." She fumbled with her document before trying to pass it over to the attendant.

He was not interested in helping her. He muttered something in German and tossed the document aside like it was a dirty handkerchief. Then he flipped the shutter down in front of his wicket, leaving her standing there, helpless. Sara sighed again and put the letter back in her bag. She realized that she didn't even know where she was going to be staying that night. Why hadn't she thought about that? Why hadn't she planned something? Why hadn't Mrs. Clifford thought to help her reserve a room somewhere for her first night? She knew it wasn't fair to blame her former boss, but how would she have known to think of these things? She had never traveled anywhere on her own. She picked up her suitcase and walked out of the building. Strangely, she didn't feel anxious like she would have in the past in the midst of something so foreign and off-putting.

Maybe she was already making progress. And maybe, deep down, behind the debilitating fatigue of this journey, she was already just a bit curious and even excited to have left the comforts of all that was familiar. The other six girls probably wouldn't even recognize me here, she thought.

Sara stared down at the document with the name and address of the doctor who had signed her medical certificate. "Well, I'm here now," she muttered. "So I'd better get on with finding out what I came to discover." There would be time to put it all together later. For now, she had to find this address and see where it led her.

Ten

THE DOOR CLICKED shut behind Sara as she entered the dimly lit house at 8 Mitterweg. It had taken her almost no time to get there from the train station. It was amazing how gestures were a universal language. She had shown a stranger the address, and with some pointing and something akin to sign language, she had been steered to this wooden house on a small dead-end street, close to the river that ran through town. Trees dotted the sidewalk. A stone path led up to the front door.

The sign out front had lifted her spirits considerably. It read *Gunther Pearlman, Doktor der Medicin*. That was the name on her certificate. She had found the place, and it appeared that the man she was searching for was still here. Things were looking up.

Inside, the front room smelled faintly of disinfectant—just like the hospital back in Hope. Sara had gotten stitches there when she cut her leg while riding on the back of Luke's motorcycle. He had loved burning rubber whenever he took her for a ride. But that day, he had taken a corner too sharply, and she had scraped her leg against some sharp bushes that jutted out into the street. It wasn't entirely Luke's fault; anyone could have misjudged the turn. But Mrs. Hazelton never forgave Luke for that one.

The front room reminded Sara of Mrs. Hazelton's cottage. A large wooden desk stood on one side, with several floral upholstered couches lined up against the wall opposite it. Sara assumed they were for patients who were waiting to see the doctor. No one was there yet. There was a fireplace on one side of the room, though it was not lit. For just a moment, Sara yearned to be back in Hope and sitting with the matron in front of her fireplace, sipping tea and talking about a dress or skirt she was thinking of sewing. Mrs. Hazelton would have nodded approvingly at Sara's design ideas—she was always so encouraging. Sara would have left her cottage eager to get to the sewing machine. But Mrs. Hazelton wasn't here, and this wasn't Hope. Sara shook those thoughts from her mind and approached the desk. She stood shifting from one foot to the other, uncertain of what to do next.

Just then a door opened at the back of the room, and a boy entered. He was tall, with short dark hair and dark-rimmed glasses that he pushed up on his nose. Kind of cute, Sara thought. He looked to be about her age. He stopped when he saw her.

"*Kann ich Ihnen helfen*?"

Sara stared at him blankly.

"*Haben Sie einen Termin*?" he continued.

"Excuse me," she replied. "I don't speak German." She shrugged her shoulders and held her hands out helplessly. "English?"

The boy eyed her curiously, and Sara felt her face grow warm. "Are you American?" he finally asked.

She breathed a sigh of relief. "I'm Canadian," she replied. "Thank goodness you speak English."

He looked amused. "I spent a couple of summers on Long Island in New York with my family. My parents insisted that I learn English—the universal language and all." He glanced at the clock on the wall. "The clinic isn't open yet. And I don't suppose you have an appointment with the doctor. That's what I was asking you."

His English was perfect. There was just a hint of a German accent there, along with something else that Sara struggled to grasp. Something familiar, but what was it? And then she remembered. He sounded like the instructor who had come to the Benevolent

Home to teach the girls ballroom dancing. What was his name? Mr. Howsham. Yes, that was it, Sara recalled. He had also come from New York, and the Seven used to laugh at the way he would ask for coffee in the dining room—it sounded more like "coo-awe-fee." This boy's English, especially when he said the words *doctor* and *Long Island* had a touch of that same accent. She found the combination interesting and appealing.

"No, I don't have an appointment, but the door was unlocked. That's why I came in," Sara continued, trying her best to remain composed. Somehow, it was important to her that she appear to really know what she was doing. Was she trying to impress him? "But I do have this."

She dug out the document with Dr. Pearlman's name written on it. She began to explain where she had gotten it, then stopped. She wasn't sure how much to tell him, this strange boy who was staring at her so intently. "Is the doctor here?" she finally asked. "I know it's early, but I've just arrived from Canada. I came straight here...I'd like to meet with him, the doctor...um...talk to him if he's available." Oh, if only she didn't hesitate so much, she would have sounded much more in control.

The boy nodded, still staring. "I'll get him. Can I ask your name? So I can tell the doctor who you are."

"Sara," she replied.

"A nice name."

Sara was taken aback and felt herself blush once more. This boy was forward, and it was making her feel uncomfortable. She began to say something else, but he interrupted her.

"Have a seat. I'll go get the doctor."

With that, he disappeared through the back door as Sara tried to steady her nerves. This boy with his intense stare and questions was more than she could take at this moment. It didn't help that she was exhausted from the journey. But now her heart was practically thumping out of her chest, making her feel light-headed. She was about to meet the doctor who had signed the certificate approving her to go to Canada. Presumably he had known her mother. And, on top of everything else, Sara was suddenly taken aback to realize that she hadn't rehearsed for this moment at all—hadn't fully believed that it was going to happen, especially this fast. She should have prepared some questions. She should have been more organized. What was she going to say to him? And more important, what would he say to her? Would he even remember who she was? Or have anything useful to offer her about her past?

She sank down onto one of the small couches, rubbed her hands together and tried to breathe deeply.

A moment later she rose when the same door opened and the boy returned, this time followed by an elderly gentleman wearing a white medical coat. He had a quick, light step despite his advanced age. He also wore glasses, the horn-rimmed kind that Mrs. Clifford wore. His hair, what was left of it, was white and encircled the back of his head like a half-moon, with only a feathery tuft on top. That part stood straight up, as if he had just been caught in a draft.

"Peter said you wanted to meet me."

Peter. It was good to know the boy's name. That way, he didn't have the upper hand. The doctor had a soft German accent, but his English was also perfect, thank goodness. Sara shook her momentary distraction with Peter and faced the doctor.

"Hello. I'm Sara—Sara Barry—from Canada. I've come over here to find you..." And then she stumbled over her words, not sure how or what to ask the doctor. Instead, she pulled out the certificate and passed it over to him.

He took the paper from her and studied it for a moment, his eyes growing wide and curious. He glanced up at Sara and then back down at the document. Finally, he extended his arm to hand it back to her. The sleeve of his lab coat pulled back to reveal a line of blue letters—no, not letters, thought Sara, trying hard not to stare. They were numbers that appeared to be tattooed on his forearm, above his wrist. Sara was perplexed. She had a vague recollection of reading something about tattooed numbers and Jewish people during the Holocaust. What was it? The doctor was speaking again.

"Yes, it's my signature on this paper," he said. "Where did you get this?"

With a deep breath, Sara launched into an explanation of her background—how she was an orphan, raised in the Benevolent Home in Hope, and how the Home had closed prematurely because of the fire and she and some of her fellow orphans had been given the opportunity to find out where they had come from. While she spoke, Peter moved over to sit behind the desk. He appeared to be studying some files that lay open on top, but out of the corner of her eye, Sara could see that he was riveted to the conversation she was having with Dr. Pearlman.

"One of the things that I was given was this note with your name and signature. I've traveled all the way from Canada to find you and talk to you about this." There! She had gotten through that part without too much trouble. If only she could stop trembling.

The doctor glanced down at the paper once more. "And you think I can somehow help you find out information about your past?"

Sara faltered. "Well, yes, I…um…thought, because you had signed this letter, that you would remember me—the baby, I mean."

"I see many babies," the doctor interrupted. He was still holding the document out to her, but Sara didn't reach for it.

"I had hoped you could give me some information about the woman who had me—my mother." Saying the word was still so strange for Sara. She was flustered, and the doctor wasn't making this easy for her. Peter appeared to have abandoned his files. He was now staring openly at her and the doctor. "I believe that she was in a concentration camp."

Dr. Pearlman sighed. "Yes, yes. Everyone came from the concentration camps back then. And I signed many certificates. I can't possibly remember every baby that I examined or every paper that I signed."

Sara tried again. "I was told that you—the doctor who signed this—had changed the information about my health. I was told I had TB as a child and that you altered the form so I would be allowed to travel. I have the name of my mother on another document." Why was she so nervous, and why was this man making this conversation so difficult? She dug through her bag for the second piece of paper, this one from the United Nations Rehabilitation and

Relief Administration. "Here," she said. "My mother's name was Karen Frankel."

She extended the paper toward the doctor, but he did not move to take it. His eyes widened again as he stared at it. "What did you say her name was?"

"Karen Frankel. You see, it's written right here." She indicated the name on the paper. "That's all I know."

Dr. Pearlman's eyes traveled from the document up to Sara's face, searching her features until his gaze came to rest on her blue eyes. He didn't say a word, though Sara could see that he had gone quite pale. Peter was standing now and also staring at the doctor.

Sara felt the hairs on her neck stand straight up. Instinctively, she stepped back out of the spotlight of his scrutiny. "I've also got this." She reached into her blouse and pulled out the Star of David necklace.

This time, Sara could see Peter leaning in to look at the star. Dr. Pearlman's gaze shifted from Sara's face to the necklace and back again. He gasped and reached up to remove his glasses. His hands were trembling; in fact, his whole body seemed to have gone into spasms. For a moment, Sara forgot about her own situation and stepped forward, reaching a hand out to rest on the doctor's arm. He did not look well.

"Are you all right? Do you want to sit down?" She couldn't imagine what had panicked him to the point of looking as if he might pass out.

Peter hurried over to stand next to Dr. Pearlman. "Herr Doktor," he said urgently. "Can I get you something?"

The doctor coughed and shook off Sara's hand. Then he turned away so that she couldn't see his face. "I can't help you," he said over his shoulder, rather brusquely this time. "I'm afraid you've come for nothing."

Sara was confused. "But you must be able to remember something—"

"No!" His voice was loud and angry.

Sara would not be deterred. "I just need you to give me some information about my mother."

"Nothing!" He was almost shouting now. "You have to leave." And with that, he strode out of the room.

Sara remained glued to the spot, staring at the empty space that had been left when the doctor stormed off. Then she turned to Peter. "What just happened?"

"I've never seen him this upset," Peter replied. He looked at Sara with brows knitted together, shaking his head.

"I didn't mean to do anything to…I just wanted some answers."

Peter nodded. "I don't understand it either."

"But I don't think I did anything wrong."

Peter jumped in quickly. "No, you didn't. There must be something else that has disturbed him."

Sara sank back down onto a couch and buried her face in her hands. This had gone worse than she could have imagined. Her stomach was aching, tied up in knots that were threatening to overcome her. If she didn't get hold of herself, she was afraid she might throw up. A pain behind her left eye began to throb, keeping time with the clock on the wall, whose second hand counted out the passing moments—one, two, three—growing with intensity until the beat became a thump. Her hands were tightly clasped. Minutes went by before she was aware that Peter had moved over to stand directly in front of her—two feet planted on the floor below her gaze. She really didn't want to talk to him, but she couldn't avoid looking up.

His face showed concern. "Are you okay?"

Sara stared at him blankly.

"What are you going to do now?"

Before Sara could even think of an answer to that question, the back door swung open and Dr. Pearlman reemerged. She jumped to her feet. The doctor had combed his tuft of hair back into place and seemed to have composed himself, though his face was still pale and he avoided looking Sara in the eye. "There is a small inn not far from here," he began. His voice was calmer as well. "Peter will take you there. It's about a fifteen-minute walk. Frau Klein, the woman who runs it, will give you a room for the night. I've already spoken to her, and she is expecting you."

Sara made a move to speak, but the doctor held up his hand to silence her.

"The inn isn't fancy, but it's clean. You can make your plans to return to Canada after you've had a night's rest."

He turned and walked out of the room, leaving Sara and Peter alone again.

Eleven

SARA WAS SILENT as she trudged after Peter on the walk to the inn. Had she really come all this way just to be told she would have to leave? No, Dr. Pearlman hadn't just asked her to leave. He had practically ordered her away. It made no sense. Sara knew that there was more to discover and that this doctor had more information than he was willing to share. Why else would he have become so unsettled and abrupt, turning on her for no reason she could comprehend? What was it that he was hiding? She had no idea how she was going to discover that.

"He's really a good man." Peter interrupted her thoughts. "The doctor—he's a caring man. All his patients say so. I've worked for him in the clinic after school and every summer for a few years now, so I know what he's like." Peter was walking just ahead of Sara. He had insisted on carrying her suitcase, despite Sara's protests. In the end, she had given in and let him take it. Pick your battles, she thought. Besides, in her weary state, she was grateful for the help. The case slapped against Peter's leg as he slowed his pace to give her a chance to catch up.

"Well, he doesn't seem to care too much about my situation," she replied. Her head was still pounding, and her stomach was still in knots over the way her conversation with Dr. Pearlman had ended. She didn't know if it was anxiety that churned in her belly or hunger. It felt as if days had gone by since her last meal.

"All that talk about the war," Peter continued. "It upsets him. That's probably why he didn't want to talk to you."

Despite her overwhelming fatigue, Sara was instantly curious. "I saw those numbers on his arm," she said. "That has something to do with this, doesn't it?"

"Those were the numbers he got when he was taken to Auschwitz. Everyone who was sent there was tattooed."

Sara recalled that Auschwitz was one of the worst of the concentration camps that Adolf Hitler had established.

"I'm told that he lost his family there—his wife, a child. He was the only one to survive," Peter continued. "When the war ended, he went to Föhrenwald—the displaced persons camp. He worked there as a doctor, trying to help other survivors."

That was the name of the place on her certificate. Föhrenwald—the place where Sara was born. The connection between her and the doctor suddenly felt as if it had intensified—another reason why he must have information about her or her mother. "How do you know all of this?" she asked Peter.

"Dr. Pearlman is a family friend. My parents also survived the camps and had me just after the war ended."

He said the word *camp* like he was talking about summer camp, not a place where people had been murdered.

"So you're Jewish!" Sara instantly regretted having blurted this out, even though Peter looked amused at the comment. "I'm sorry," she continued quickly. "I don't mean to be so personal, but you have to know that this is all so new to me. I've never actually met anyone Jewish. Well, that's not quite true. There was a Jewish minister who came to speak once at our church back home."

"You mean a rabbi," Peter interrupted.

Sara felt her face redden again. "Of course! A rabbi." She exhaled before continuing. "Anyway, this rabbi came to speak at our church in Hope—the town that I'm from. He talked about some Jewish customs. But I have to admit, I didn't really pay too much attention. And now I wish I had! I guess I've got a lot to learn about all of this."

"Well, in answer to your question, yes, I'm Jewish. There aren't that many of us living here now—not many who stayed in Germany after the war. So many of those who survived were eager to get away from this country. Those of us who are left are a bit of a tight-knit community. Frau Klein who runs the inn is a survivor as well."

They arrived at their destination—a charming A-frame chalet with colorful wooden carvings across its gables, and flower pots that lined the walkway up to the brightly painted red door. The sign out front read *Landhaus Inn*. Peter knocked and waited. A few minutes later they heard shuffling feet on the other side, and an older woman answered. She had the gentlest face Sara had ever seen. There was no other way to describe it—warm eyes that invited you in and a smile that threatened to stretch up to the tops of her ears. Frau Klein felt like kindness personified—tender and embracing. And all of that was contained in the tiniest of frames. She couldn't have been much more than four feet tall, but she was impeccably dressed, as if she took great pride in always looking her best. Her silver hair was pulled up into a fashionable beehive-shaped bun at the back of her head. And she stood straight and strong despite her years, which Sara guessed to be even more than Dr. Pearlman's. Sara liked her immediately.

"Sara, this is Frau Klein. Unfortunately, she doesn't speak English. I assume the doctor explained your situation to her on the telephone. But I'll just fill her in and help you get settled. Then you'll be on your own." Peter proceeded to speak rapid-fire German to Frau Klein while Sara looked on. The elderly woman continued to smile and nod, cooing ever so slightly under her breath as Peter presumably talked about the events that had unfolded at the doctor's office. Finally, she reached up and lightly stroked Sara's cheek. Her hands were chapped and raw, as if she had soaked them in harsh laundry detergent over a lifetime. But the gentleness of the gesture took Sara's breath away, and her eyes instantly filled with tears. She was not used to being touched with such unreserved affection. Frau Klein continued to coo and cluck as Peter finished talking. It was only then that Sara noticed the tattooed numbers on Frau Klein's arm as well. In one day, Sara had met two survivors of the Holocaust—more than she had ever imagined meeting in her lifetime!

Sara shook hands with Frau Klein and then stood there in the entranceway, awkwardly waiting for something to happen. Just then a black-and-white, short-haired dog waddled in from another room and walked up to Sara, sinking to the floor and nestling up against her foot. It was some kind of a mongrel, a mixture of breeds that Sara couldn't begin to figure out. And it was almost as wide as it was long.

"Ah, this is Frau Klein's pride and joy," said Peter, bending to scratch the mutt behind its ear.

Sara was usually not one to take to dogs. She didn't hate them, and she certainly wasn't afraid. She just hadn't been around them enough to get used to them or warm up to them.

"His name is John Wayne. Frau Klein loves American westerns," he added when he saw Sara's amused look. Frau Klein said something in German, and Peter smiled. "She says that John Wayne is probably as old as she is, and just as...what's a word that you use to describe someone who isn't afraid to go after what they want?"

"Determined?" Sara replied.

"Even more than that."

"Gutsy!"

"Yes, that's a better word. John Wayne is gutsy." As if on cue, the dog responded with a quick bark, struggling to his feet and wagging his tail.

Sara knelt down to give the dog a pat on his head. John Wayne immediately leaned forward to lick her on the cheek. She was delighted and instantly taken with him.

Frau Klein spoke to Peter again.

"He must like you," said Peter. "Frau Klein says he is quite stingy with his affection."

Sara stared at the dog panting in front of her. I could use a friend right now, she thought. Even a four-legged one. "You're a sweet old dog, you know that?" she said.

John Wayne tilted his head to one side and raised an ear.

"I'm afraid he also only understands German," said Peter. "*Sitz*!" he commanded. The dog fell back on his haunches. Then Peter said something else and John Wayne lifted a fat paw and placed it in Sara's hand. That sealed their friendship.

"Well, it looks like you don't need me anymore," said Peter. "Between Frau Klein and John Wayne, I think you'll be well taken care of." He handed Sara her suitcase and turned to go. "I'll come back tomorrow and take you to the train station to make arrangements to get back to Canada."

Sara rose from the floor and began to protest. She had gotten here on her own, and she wouldn't need any help getting back. Besides, she was not used to boys doing things for her. Back in Hope, she'd had to remind Luke to hold the door open for her. Not that she had needed that either! But then she stopped herself. There was something about Peter that she liked. And yes, in the midst of this strange and foreign country, perhaps a little help was just what she was going to need.

Twelve

THE ROOM THAT Frau Klein led Sara up to was bright and inviting. Its walls were covered in floral wallpaper, and a matching eiderdown comforter lay across the four-poster bed. It was one of the prettiest rooms Sara had ever seen. While she, Dot and Tess had tried to create a welcoming space in the small room they had shared at the orphanage, their dorm room had always felt plain and sterile. This one felt like a warm summer day. She flopped down onto the bed, wondering again when the last time was that she had slept; she figured it was more than a day ago. And yet, oddly, she wasn't ready to close her eyes. Frau Klein had insisted that she eat something before going to her room, and Sara had gladly consented. Now, with food in her belly and energy pumping through her body, she was wide awake and buzzing with thoughts. She needed to sort them out and began to make a mental list of the things she knew so far.

1. Dr. Pearlman. He was abrupt and perhaps even rude. And he was certainly mysterious. Peter insisted that the doctor was kind, but so far Sara had not seen any evidence of that.

2. Peter. He was interesting and definitely eager to lend a helping hand. And Sara had to admit that she found him attractive. But it was crazy for her to even think about anything else. She had just ended a relationship with someone she thought she had known, someone who had turned out to be a disaster. And she was finally moving forward. Now was definitely not the time to think about guys.

3. Her journey. Was it about to end almost before it had started? She didn't want to leave Germany yet, though Dr. Pearlman had made it clear that she should get on the next train out of Wolfratshausen. There had to be a way for her to discover something about her parents. This was the location that the documents all pointed to. This was where she had come from.

4. Everything seemed to lead back to the mysterious Dr. Pearlman. He had seemed quite interested and polite at first, yet cut her off so quickly

once she showed him the certificate with his signature. Why?

Just before going up to her room, Sara had managed to convey to Frau Klein that she wanted to look at a local telephone book. Even though she knew it was fruitless, she had searched through it to see if she could find a listing for the name Karen Frankel. Just as she thought, there were no names close to that. She presumed her mother must have been dying when she sent Sara away. But a small part of her wondered if maybe—just maybe—there was a chance her mother was still alive. But if that were true, then why would her mother have abandoned her? Did it have something to do with her father—whoever he was? She had no information about him whatsoever. Sara sighed aloud in the empty room. She had barely been here for a day and already she had more questions than she had arrived with—along with a couple of dead ends!

She reached into her purse, pulled out her wallet and began to count out how much money was left. Mrs. Hazelton's contribution of $138 had pretty much taken care of the round-trip airfare. That left Sara with her own nest egg of nearly $300. The inn was only $10 a night, with two meals that Frau Klein would provide. And if the snack she had just eaten was any indication, Sara knew she would be well fed. So she still had plenty of cash for this trip. She had a return ticket in one week's time. Why go home now? For a moment she wondered what Mrs. Hazelton would say if she knew the situation Sara was in. Well, she didn't have to think about that for more than a second. Sara knew that the matron would urge her to continue searching—not to give up. Mrs. Hazelton's words of advice—*Sometimes you need to look back in order to move forward*—echoed loudly in Sara's head.

She rose, lugged her suitcase onto the bed and opened it, staring down at the clothes neatly folded inside. Just before leaving Hope, she had managed to sew a couple of skirts and blouses, using Mrs. Clifford's sewing machine. Her former boss had even given her the fabric, claiming she had piles of it at home. *You'll put it to better use today than I could in a dozen years*, she'd insisted. The pieces Sara had whipped up fit her much better than the clothes she had been given at the church after the fire.

Without even thinking, she began to remove the items, one by one. She hung her skirts and pants in the small closet next to the bed and piled the sweaters and undergarments into the wooden chest of drawers on the other side of the room. Then she laid the copy of *The Diary of Anne Frank* on the small table next to her bed. It didn't take her long to empty the suitcase, which she placed in another corner.

With that done, Sara plopped down on the bed once more and stared out the window. It was starting to get dark, and the last rays of the setting sun cast a yellow glow into her room. There was a robin's nest to one side of her windowsill, securely nestled under one of the gables. Four little heads poked out of the nest, mouths open to the sky, waiting expectantly. Suddenly, as if on cue, the mother robin appeared with a worm dangling from her beak. The four heads stretched higher toward the mother bird, demanding to be fed. These babies were big and plump and threatened to spill out of the nest in their eagerness to be the first to get to the food. Just like the Little Ones back at the orphanage, Sara thought, smiling to herself. The mother robin pushed the worm into the mouths of a couple of her babies and then flew off again to search for more food. Sara watched the mother bird taking care of her babies and wondered, briefly, why her own mother had never done the same for her. It was a ridiculous comparison; she knew that. But she couldn't help going there in her mind. Why had she been abandoned? Would she ever discover the reason? As she watched the babies bob up and down, waiting for their mother to reappear, she laid her head down on the comforter, closed her eyes and in seconds was fast asleep.

She awoke slowly, hours later, in the exact same spot, in the same clothes in which she had arrived. She had been dreaming that she was back in her dorm room at the orphanage, with Dot and Tess in the beds across from her. Joe was cooking downstairs, and the smell of eggs and toast was drifting up to her room. Soon Miss Webster would begin knocking on the doors of all the orphans, signaling them to get up and get ready for chores and breakfast. For a moment, Sara allowed herself to stay there, comforted by an image that was familiar and felt safe. Then she began to stretch and slowly opened her eyes, taking a moment to orient herself to her surroundings. Her head felt thick and filled with cobwebs. But slowly the floral wallpaper came into focus, and she knew she was not in Hope. She was in Frau Klein's inn, waking up to her second day in Germany. The smell of breakfast being prepared below wafted up to fill her room. With a deep sigh, Sara knew it was time to get up.

She rose, but not before she had turned to the window to check on the baby robins. All appeared to be quiet there for now. Then she went to shower and change her clothes, putting on one of the blouses she had made before leaving Hope. Finally, she made her way down to the kitchen, where Frau Klein was busy making breakfast. The smell was heavenly, and Sara realized that she was famished.

"Good morning," she said.

"*Guten Morgen*." Frau Klein smiled and guided Sara to the table, where she presented her with platters of eggs, toast, fried potatoes and a delicious thick yogurt with fresh fruit. All this was to be washed down with strong coffee and hot milk. Sara hadn't had a feast like this in a long time. Just as she was digging in, John Wayne entered the kitchen from outside. When he saw Sara, his tail began to wag furiously, practically throwing him off his feet. His ample behind swayed from side to side as he wobbled over to sit next to her chair.

"Good morning, John Wayne," she said, reaching down to scratch behind his ear. He closed his eyes and leaned into her hand.

At that moment, Frau Klein placed the dog's bowl of food in a corner of the kitchen. John Wayne didn't wait for an invitation. He pranced over to bury his face in his own breakfast.

From the size of him, he looked like he'd had his share of Frau Klein's cooking, Sara thought, amused.

And she could understand his enthusiasm. Frau Klein continued to bring plate after plate of food to Sara. "*Komm, iss, komm, iss!!*" the innkeeper insisted. Sara knew without really understanding that she was being urged to eat. She lifted her fork and began to dig in. Even though she could barely communicate with Frau Klein about anything, there was no awkwardness in their interaction. They smiled at one another, nodded, and every once in a while, Frau Klein would squeeze Sara's arm and mutter something in German. Sara just grinned back and continued eating.

She was just finishing her second freshly baked cinnamon roll when the door opened and Peter entered. He sat down opposite her without being invited and leaned forward. "Hello. You're looking well rested."

She looked away self-consciously and pulled on her ponytail. Why did he fluster her so much? Instead of responding, she pointed to the cinnamon roll she was enjoying. "This is so good," she said.

"It's called a *Schnecke*," Peter replied as Frau Klein set one down in front of him. Sara laughed at the strange-sounding word. "You'll think it's even funnier when I tell you what it means," Peter added through a mouthful of bun. "*Schnecke* is the German word for snail, which is what we think this bun is shaped like.

Laugh all you want," he added. "People line up to buy them from Frau Klein. She must like you a lot." Frau Klein continued to smile and hover in the background as Sara and Peter talked.

"I can't remember the last time I ate this much food," Sara said, reaching for another schnecke and setting it down on her plate. "But I have to ask you, where are all the other people? I haven't seen anyone else. I thought this was an inn."

"You're the only guest staying here right now. But the truth is, this is a small town, and not many people pass through. It gets a lot busier in the summer, but this is still early in the season."

"It's just like where I come from. There's a fishing derby that brings people out in the summer, along with the bird watchers. But other than that, my hometown is as quiet as this place. But does that mean that Frau Klein made all of this just for me?" The breakfast was enough for a banquet.

"She doesn't need much of an excuse to cook." He pointed at the platters in front of them. "There are two things that make Frau Klein happy—cooking for people, and watching them eat. Besides, as I said, I think she likes you. She doesn't really have any relatives left. Her husband was killed in the camps, and they had no children. The other Jewish families try to watch out for her, though you can see that she's strong and quite independent. She's kind of like everyone's substitute grandmother."

Frau Klein motioned for Sara to have some more. She shook her head gratefully and pushed her plate away. "Tell her I'm going to explode if I have another bite."

Frau Klein laughed as Peter translated. Sara wondered briefly how this woman, who had clearly lost so much in the war, could continue to smile and reach out so lovingly to those around her. Sara could learn a lot from Frau Klein's example.

Peter was still polishing off his cinnamon roll. "Is your suitcase packed?" he asked through a full mouth. "Would you like me to go upstairs and get it?"

Sara rose from the table and began to bring dishes to the sink. She turned to face Peter. "My plans have changed. I'm not going anywhere for a while." She explained about having a return ticket one week from today, and about how she needed to spend more time trying to figure out the puzzle of her birth. "Besides, there's no reason for me to go back to Hope. I really don't have anything there."

It was Peter's turn to push his plate away. "*Nein, danke*," he said, shaking his head when Frau Klein tried to give him another bun. He stared over at Sara. "What do you think you're going to find here?"

"I don't know. But I've come all this way to search for my mother. If Dr. Pearlman isn't going to help me, then I've got to try something else. I'm not ready to give up yet."

There was a long pause as Peter also rose and began to help clear the dishes. Frau Klein was busy wrapping the leftovers in smaller bowls. John Wayne was still loudly crunching his breakfast in the background. Finally, Peter turned to Sara. "I'll help you, if you'd like."

Sara turned away, not wanting to show how relieved she was at the offer. At this point, she still didn't want to rely on Peter—or anyone, for that matter. But she knew that she could certainly use his help, if for no other reason than to be her guide and translator. That was as much as she was prepared to admit for the time being, even though, deep down inside of her, there was the stirring of something else. She pushed that thought far away.

"Thank you," she replied, keeping her voice even. "I think I could use the help."

Thirteen

PETER SMILED. "SO, where would you like to start?"

"Here," Sara said as she pulled out the medical document that she had slipped into her pocket. "It says here that I was born in Föhrenwald. You told me it's where Dr. Pearlman also went after the war. Maybe if I go there, I'll find something or someone who can help me."

Peter studied the document. "It's not far from here. We can bicycle there. Frau Klein will lend us the bikes." He said something in German to the innkeeper and then glanced out the window. "It's sunny right now, but I know it's supposed to rain later today. I hope you don't mind getting wet."

Frau Klein pointed to the sky and responded in German.

"She says that the sun must have come out just for you this morning. She says that the blue sky matches your eyes."

Sara blushed and tugged at her ponytail again, while Frau Klein laughed and said something else to Peter. This time it was his face that reddened.

"What did she say?"

Peter shook his head. "Frau Klein thinks she's a matchmaker. I'll just leave it at that."

Frau Klein's laughter followed them out the door and into the shed, where Peter located the bikes under a gray canvas oilcloth. While Sara wiped one of them down, Peter began to fill the tires of the other using a pump he found nearby.

"I'm afraid the bikes haven't been touched all winter," he said. "But it won't take long to get them ready." They worked side by side until Peter broke the silence again. "I must ask you about your name—Sara Barry. It's not a very...Jewish-sounding name."

Sara laughed. She knew it wasn't even her real last name, just the one that Mrs. Hazelton had given her upon her arrival at the orphanage. She explained this to Peter. "Our matron liked to name the girls after characters in the books by the authors she loved the most—Chaucer, Brontë, Mitchell. But she kept her favorite book for me and the six other older girls in the house—my best friends," she added. "Our last names came from *Anne of Green Gables*. Have you heard of that book?"

"Yes," Peter replied. "But it's not one that I've read."

"It was written by Lucy Maud Montgomery. Mrs. Hazelton said that even though I was recovering from TB when I arrived at the orphanage, I was such a round child—*cheeks exploding across my face*, she used to say. It reminded her of Anne's best friend, Diana Barry, who she said was also rather plump. I never really questioned it," she added. "I was always just Sara Barry." Luke had sometimes made fun of the name, Sara recalled. He'd called her *Hairy Barry*, or *Cherry Barry*, which she hated. She didn't tell Peter that part. "My mother's last name was Frankel. So I guess that's my real last name, unless there's more to this puzzle than I thought."

They set out, riding side by side out of Wolfratshausen and south toward Föhrenwald. The sandwiches Frau Klein had insisted on packing for them were in a container in the basket of Sara's bicycle. It was a clear, warm day. And although Sara could detect dark clouds gathering on the horizon, she couldn't believe they would turn into anything more menacing.

The sky above her was too bright. The morning sun was welcoming as it pitched its rays across the town. Sara pumped her legs up and down on the pedals, enjoying the exercise, reminded of the days she used to bicycle to work at Loretta's.

Eventually Peter took the lead, and Sara fell in behind him, following closely as he wove through the streets of Wolfratshausen and then turned away from the river to follow a smaller road south. Here, the houses were separated by larger patches of green land. The sun played hide-and-seek in the tree branches that hung low over the road. The road itself was unpaved and rough, and her bicycle wheels rattled and bounced underneath her. After only about fifteen minutes, Peter began to slow down, and Sara did the same. They were approaching a residential area, and the road was beginning to smooth out once more. Ahead of her, Sara could see homes and buildings lining both sides of the street. There were several office buildings, a church and a school. Children were gathered in the playground, running across the pavement and squealing as they passed one another. Peter pulled over by the side of the road. He gestured around him.

"I told you it wasn't far. This is Föhrenwald."

Sara glanced around. She wasn't sure what she had been expecting, but this wasn't exactly it.

This looked like one of the neighborhoods back in Hope, not a place that had once housed Jews who had survived the Holocaust.

"You look puzzled," said Peter.

"Are you sure this is it?" Sara asked. "I mean, are you sure this was the displaced persons camp?" Was she looking for evidence of suffering? Or death? Of course, that was ridiculous. The war had ended years ago.

Peter nodded. "This is it. My parents told me a lot about this place." He went on to explain that at one time there had been over 5,000 Jewish refugees living here. "There were dormitories and small apartments, there and there." He pointed. "There was a school, probably smaller than this one, a library, a hospital and even a synagogue."

"But where is all of that now?"

"A lot of the original buildings were torn down when the DP camp closed in 1957. That's when all of these smaller homes were built. Now it's really just a..." He struggled to find the word. "What do you call a place that is part of a city, but just outside?"

"A suburb?" Sara offered.

Peter nodded. "Yes, that's it. Föhrenwald is a suburb of Wolfratshausen. Everything's changed in the last few years. It's not even called Föhrenwald anymore. Now the place is called Waldram. Even the street signs are different," he said, indicating a pole with a rather new-looking banner on it. "My parents told me that the streets used to be named for people and states in America. This corner was once called Roosevelt and Pennsylvania."

Sara looked up at the street sign. They were at the corner of Thomasstrasse and Faulhaberstrasse. "Why did they change everything?"

"Once this place closed, everyone tried their hardest to forget about the past. There was, and is, such shame associated with the concentration camps in this country and what the Nazis did to the Jews. If people could change what this place was called, perhaps they could erase what it once was."

Sara was silent. She understood the desire to try to cover up the past, or to forget about who you were and where you had come from. But here she was, trying to do exactly the opposite—she was trying to uncover her past. How was she going to do that if everything had changed or been wiped out? She needed to find out what was once here. She needed to see if anyone knew or could remember her mother. There was only one way to do that. Sara climbed off her bicycle, flipped the kickstand down and began to walk up the stone path leading to one of the small houses. Peter quickly parked his bike and ran up the path to stop her.

"What are you doing?" he asked, reaching out to grab her arm.

"I want to talk to someone," replied Sara. "I want to see if anyone can give me information about my mother."

"I've got to warn you," he cautioned. "Some of the people around here may not be so willing to talk to you."

"Why not?"

Peter cast his eyes downward. He looked uncomfortable. "As I said, people around here have been trying to forget the past. What Germany did to the Jews of Europe is a"—he searched for the word—"a stain on this country, a crime that shocked the world. The families who lived in this area at that time don't want to admit that they may have seen what was happening and yet did nothing to try and stop it. Some may even have helped!"

"But I'm not blaming them."

"No," Peter continued. "And many were simply too scared for themselves to do anything at that time. They may have hated what was going on and yet still could do nothing to stop it. But even that is something they would prefer to forget."

Sara hesitated. And as she stood on the pathway, with dark clouds approaching from the distance, she had a fleeting memory of what Luke had done to Malou back in Hope. How he had harassed her and called her horrible names—and how Sara had ignored it. She was determined to be better than that from now on. Besides, Mrs. Hazelton had said that she needed to look back in order to get on with her life. Maybe the people of this place needed to do the same. This feeling of purpose was all new to her, and it was pretty fleeting. Sara stared back at Peter. She knew that if she blinked, she might lose her nerve, and she needed all of it to push forward. Then she pulled herself free of his grasp.

"I understand what you're saying. But I have to try this," she said as she approached the front door of the house. With only a brief hesitation, she reached up and knocked.

Within seconds, an elderly woman answered. She appeared to be about Frau Klein's age and had the same worn hands and wrinkled face. She wore a colorful scarf tied around her head and a matching apron around her waist. She glanced at Peter and stared suspiciously at Sara's Star of David, which had freed itself from her blouse in the ride here. "*Ja*?" she asked.

Sara turned helplessly to Peter. "Please!" she begged. "I need you to translate." Reluctantly, he approached the door and stood next to Sara. "Tell her that my mother lived in this place when it was a DP camp. Tell her I'm looking for someone who might have known her or seen her."

As Peter began to talk, the old woman's eyes narrowed and darkened. She said something harshly. Sara didn't need the translation to know that she was angry.

"She said she had nothing to do with what went on back then," Peter began.

Sara urged him on. "Tell her that I understand that, but I just want some information."

The woman said something else, just as harshly, and Peter looked even more helpless. "She says she doesn't know anything about that time."

Sara would not be stopped. "Tell her I've got this document with my mother's name on it." Sara began to dig in her bag for the paper to show the woman. But before she could find it, the woman barked out one more statement and then slammed the door with a loud bang.

"She said to leave her alone," Peter said.

Sara looked around, undeterred. "Well, that was only one house. There are plenty more to try." With that, Sara approached a second house, where another elderly woman greeted her with the same response. At house after house they got the same reaction. After each attempt, Peter trailed farther behind, ever more reluctant to question the people of the town. Sara thought she might have some luck with a younger man who opened his door and listened politely as Peter filled in Sara's story. But it turned out that he had just moved to this neighborhood from Berlin. He knew nothing of the town's past.

"At least he didn't slam the door in our faces," said Sara. But she still had no information. At the fifth or sixth house—she was beginning to lose count—the man who answered the door came out with his cane raised above his head and waved it threateningly in Sara's direction. She and Peter backed away.

"Let's just say that he wants us off his property," Peter replied when Sara pushed him for the translation.

The sky had become heavy with the possibility of showers. And the clouds that had hovered in the distance were now directly above Sara's head. By the time she had tried three more houses, with the same results, fat drops of rain were beginning to fall.

"I think we need to get out of here," Peter said. "This is only going to get worse."

The rain, which began as erratic drops, quickly became a strong and steady downpour. Sara and Peter bolted toward the street to where they had left their bicycles. The wind gathered strength, whipping the spray into Sara's face as she reluctantly climbed onto her bicycle and followed Peter back to Wolfratshausen. She was completely disheartened and confused by the ugly reaction of the townspeople of Föhrenwald, and her spirits had turned as murky as the sky, which had gone from dazzling blue to gray and bleak.

This was not the way Sara had imagined the day unfolding. She had thought she was going to uncover some piece of her past, something that connected her to this place and these people. She had thought she was going to find a piece of herself here. Instead, she had gone from feeling like an outsider as an orphan in Hope to feeling like even more of one here in Germany. Instead of finding the place where she belonged, she was finding herself to be more of an outcast than ever.

Fourteen

BY THE TIME Sara and Peter had ridden their bikes back to Wolfratshausen, they were drenched. Sara's hair hung in wet ringlets around her face, and her clothes clung to her body. Peter was just as soaked. Sara could tell that he was trying hard not to stare at her as they stashed their bikes in the shed and entered the back of the inn. Sara was carrying the basket of uneaten sandwiches that Frau Klein had prepared earlier that morning. In the confusion and disappointment of the day, there had been no opportunity to stop and eat. Besides, their outing had been much shorter than Sara had anticipated. She wasn't at all hungry. However, she assumed she would face a lot of questions from Frau Klein, who would not be happy that they had failed to eat her snack. Surprisingly, all was quiet when they entered the inn.

"That's funny," Peter began, almost reading Sara's thoughts.

"I know," Sara replied. "Where's Frau Klein? And where's John Wayne?" At least the dog should have been there to greet them.

"Maybe she's gone out to meet someone." Peter glanced out the window. The rain was still coming down in sheets. "But with this weather, I don't know why she would have left." He was trying not to appear worried, but Sara could see it on his face. Puddles were forming at their feet.

"We have to dry off," she said, trying to avoid his look.

Rummaging around in a cupboard, Sara managed to find a couple of old towels, which she handed to Peter. Then she ran up to her room to change out of her wet clothing. She didn't want to think about the possibility of anything having happened to Frau Klein. Even though she had just met the elderly woman, Sara already felt an emotional connection to her that was stronger than she had felt for any grown-up, except maybe Mrs. Hazelton, and even that was different. Mrs. Hazelton was proper and formal. Frau Klein was soft-hearted and sentimental—*like everyone's substitute grandmother*, Peter had said. The tender feeling was new for Sara, but she liked it.

She pulled on a dry sweater and pants and quickly towel-dried her hair. Outside her window, the robins' heads were jutting up into the sky, searching for food. But when Sara looked closer, she realized there were only three babies there and not the four she had seen the previous day. The mother robin was perched in a tree nearby and was cheeping loudly, calling out to her babies to join her. They must be ready to fly off, Sara realized. One must have already left the nest. Soon they would all be gone, just as it was meant to be.

Sara left her room and began to walk down the stairs. The lights were out in the sitting room, and the curtains drawn. That too was odd. When Sara had passed this room earlier in the morning, the curtains had been wide-open, and the sun was streaming in. She wondered why Frau Klein had darkened the room like this. She was just about to go back into the kitchen to find Peter when she heard a sound from across the room—a low, broken moan, like someone crying but trying to muffle it. Sara peered around, trying to make out the hazy shapes. And that was when she saw her. Frau Klein was sitting in a big armchair, folded forward as if she had collapsed. Her face was buried in her hands as she rocked back and forth.

Sara flew across the room, calling out as she ran, "Peter! In here! Something's happened to Frau Klein!"

Sara reached the elderly woman and knelt at her feet, reaching up to place her hands on the woman's shoulders. Frau Klein jumped and looked at Sara. Her eyes were red and puffy. Her smile had evaporated. Dread and fear were written across her face. Sara felt her heart grow cold. But before she could say a word, Peter was on the floor by her side. He began speaking urgently, a string of German words that were meaningless to Sara. Frau Klein responded in a low, strained voice while tears gathered in her eyes and spilled down onto her cheeks. Sara felt helpless crouched on the floor. If only she understood what was going on.

"Is she sick? Should we call a doctor? Take her to the hospital?" It had been a couple of days since Sara's anxiety had gotten the better of her. But now she began grinding her hands together with rapid motions.

Peter exchanged a few more words with Frau Klein. Then he sat back on his heels and turned to Sara. "It's John Wayne," he said.

"The dog?"

Peter nodded. "It happened fast, just after we left this morning. John Wayne lay down on the kitchen floor. Frau Klein thought he was sleeping—he always takes a nap after breakfast. But when she went to look at him a short while later, he was breathing badly and wouldn't wake up when she tried to move him."

At first Sara was relieved—she had been terrified that this dear, sweet woman was sick, maybe even dying. And even though they were still relative strangers, the thought of losing Frau Klein had saddened her completely. But the relief was short-lived, seeing how distraught Frau Klein was.

"She loves that dog more than anything," Peter continued. "If something happens to John Wayne..." He stopped before finishing the sentence.

Sara gulped. She knew that, especially after having lost everyone in the war, Frau Klein thought of John Wayne as family, as important as a child or a sibling. "Is he going to be okay?" she asked.

"They told Frau Klein at the animal clinic that they needed to run some more tests." Peter looked up at Sara. "But it doesn't sound good."

The telephone rang and Peter went to answer it while Sara continued to try and comfort Frau Klein. When Peter returned, his face was ashen. He bent down to Frau Klein and whispered something to her. She cried out again as Sara stroked her back, desperately trying to soothe the old lady.

"Tell me what's going on," cried Sara.

Peter hesitated before responding. "That was the clinic." His eyes locked with Sara's, and she understood in that moment that the situation with John Wayne was critical.

"We need to do something," Sara said. "Is there some way we can help her?"

"The vet is going to give John Wayne a shot," Peter said. "Frau Klein wants to go back to the clinic to stay with him...until the end. The vet's office isn't far from here."

Sara jumped to her feet. "Yes, let's go with her. She shouldn't be on her own."

She helped Frau Klein to her feet and ran to get a shawl for her, which she wrapped around her shoulders. The rain had eased up considerably. Now it was just a light drizzle. But Peter grabbed a large umbrella from the front closet, and with Frau Klein on one arm and the umbrella in his other hand, he escorted her out the door. Sara took up a position on the other side of the innkeeper. The three walked down the street, arms linked. There was no conversation.

Sara was lost in her own thoughts. She realized that she had forgotten all about the trip to Föhrenwald that had happened earlier. All the disappointment at not finding anyone who could give her information about her own mother had been replaced with the concern she was feeling for Frau Klein. She glanced over at Peter. His eyes were on Frau Klein, and his face was strained and pale. Sara was struck by the compassion he clearly felt for his elderly friend.

He was probably kinder than any guy she had ever met, she realized.

When they reached the clinic, they were quickly ushered in to see John Wayne. He was lying on a small table, panting heavily, eyes closed. Frau Klein approached him and began to gently stroke his head and his body, whispering in his ear and pressing her face to his fur. Sara didn't have to know what she was saying to understand what was going on. Frau Klein was saying goodbye.

"The vet has already given him a shot," Peter said. "He says it won't be long." After several more minutes had passed, Peter added, "I don't think I can watch. I'm going to wait in the other room."

Sara nodded. It was hard to be here and witness the anguish of this moment. But after her breakdown at the inn, Frau Klein was very composed and calm. Sara marveled at how she had found that strength. She didn't want to leave Frau Klein alone and wanted to show that she could be strong for her. "I'll stay here," she replied, gulping hard to keep herself from crying.

As soon as Peter had left the room, Sara approached the table to stand next to Frau Klein. She scratched behind John Wayne's ear and bent down to bring her face close to his head.

"Hello, you sweet old thing," she whispered. At the sound of her voice, John Wayne opened one eye. His tail slowly lifted off the table, and his tongue slipped out of his mouth to lick Sara on the cheek. Then he lowered his tail and closed his eyes once more. Sara and Frau Klein continued to stand over John Wayne as his breathing became shallower and his chest rose and fell more slowly. Finally, his body became still and they knew that he was gone.

Peter, Sara and Frau Klein walked back to the inn in silence. As soon as they arrived, Frau Klein began to busy herself in the kitchen, removing plates of food from the refrigerator and bringing them over to the table where Sara and Peter sat. Somehow, they managed to convince the elderly woman to sit with them. Peter brought her tea in a tall glass and set it down in front of her. She squeezed lemon into the hot liquid. Steam rose in gently winding streams as Frau Klein lifted the glass with trembling hands to take a sip. But within minutes, she was back on her feet and bringing more food to the table. There was no point in trying to stop her. Sara understood that it was comforting and probably distracting to Frau Klein to feed the young people. And so they simply watched as she loaded the table with food and urged them to eat.

"I don't understand how this happened so fast," Sara finally said to break the unbearable silence. "When we left here this morning, John Wayne seemed fine."

"I spoke to the vet while you were in the room with Frau Klein. He told me that the dog had been sick for some time—something in his lungs that wasn't going to get better. And he was old. I think his system couldn't handle it anymore and just shut down. Frau Klein didn't think it would happen this fast, but apparently she knew it was coming."

At the mention of her name, Frau Klein smiled at Sara and said something to Peter.

Sara looked up at the innkeeper. "Is she going to be all right?"

"She said she's fine and she'll get through this. She also said she's grateful that she could be with John Wayne when he took his last breath," replied Peter. "And she wants to thank you for being at her side. It was pretty brave," Peter added. "That last part is from me."

Sara gulped hard. She had never in her life felt brave about anything. She and Peter remained at the table, trying to please Frau Klein by eating as much food as they could, even though they had little appetite.

Peter finally got up to leave, but not before promising that he would be back the next day.

"I've got to do some work for Dr. Pearlman in the morning. But I'll be here as soon as I'm done."

Sara felt reassured to know that. She watched as Frau Klein gave Peter a big hug and followed it with one for her. Then Sara climbed the stairs to her room.

Once inside she sat at the small desk that was next to the bed. She fingered the Star of David around her neck and turned it up to her face so that she could look at it. She still didn't know what the letters across the front meant. Peter had said that the writing was in Hebrew. He didn't know more than that. Sara let the necklace rest back on her chest and reached into the desk drawer, pulling out a pen and a sheet of writing paper. It had a small black-and-white drawing of the Landhaus Inn in one corner. She stared down at it and then picked up the pen and began to write.

Dear Dot,

I've been here in Germany for a couple of days now. The weather has been on and off—sometimes sunny, but sometimes so rainy that it's soaked me to the skin.

She stopped and stared at what she had just written. Who cares about the weather, she thought.

Just get to the point. With a deep breath, she began again.

This has been harder for me than I had thought it would be. I thought it would be simple to find out some things about my mother, and then I'd be on a plane coming home. That's not the way things have worked out. I haven't found anyone who is willing to talk to me, let alone tell me anything important. I'm beginning to think there may be nothing to find out. Maybe this will all be a waste of time as far as that's concerned. Maybe I'll never know where I came from. I've felt as if I don't belong anywhere—not in Hope, and not here in Germany.

Sara paused for a moment and then continued writing.

I really don't want to sound like I'm complaining. And not everything is as terrible as it sounds. I've met some people here—people who are kind and take care of each other. And even though they've had some impossibly hard things to deal with themselves, they have reached out to try and take care of me too. I don't understand a lot of what some of them are saying, but that doesn't seem to matter. I said I didn't think I would feel as if I belonged here, but I guess that's not entirely true. I guess I'm realizing that you belong wherever you feel cared for.

Sara paused again, surprised at herself for having written that last sentence.

I miss you and I hope you are well. I hope you are finding out important things about your past. I haven't done any sewing here, but I haven't forgotten our pact. I hope you don't forget it either.

She signed the letter, folded it into an envelope she found in the drawer and then got ready for bed.

Fifteen

SHE HADN'T MEANT to sleep so late. She had wanted to get up early and be downstairs helping Frau Klein or simply keeping her company. But when Sara finally rolled over in bed and opened her eyes, the sun was pouring into her room from midway across the sky. She dressed quickly, grabbed her letter to Dot and ran down the stairs. Frau Klein was in the kitchen at the counter, elbow deep in some kind of pastry dough. Her hands were pounding the mixture up and down so hard and fast that the loose skin above her elbows waved back and forth like a flag in the wind. But when she saw Sara, she wiped her hands quickly on her apron and motioned for Sara to sit and have something to eat. Sara smiled and shook her head, indicating that she would only have some coffee. She had to find a way to fight Frau Klein's over-zealous cooking without offending the woman. At this rate, it would not be long before the clothes Sara had made for herself before coming here would no longer fit her! She tried not to be moved by the disappointed look on Frau Klein's face. She grabbed a cup of coffee and sat down at the kitchen table. Frau Klein placed a slice of apple cake next to her cup. Sara sighed. How could she resist?

Frau Klein returned to her baking while Sara picked away at the cake. It was quiet in the kitchen, and Sara found herself missing John Wayne, who would have planted himself next to her, panting heavily and hoping for some crumbs from her plate to fall his way. His food and water dishes were still sitting on the floor in the corner of the kitchen, as if Frau Klein couldn't bear to remove them yet. It would be the final acknowledgment that he was gone. Sara yearned to say something to Frau Klein. This was one of those moments when the language barrier was so frustrating. She wanted to ask how the innkeeper was feeling after her terrible loss of the day before. She wanted to offer some words of consolation and support. She wanted to say that she was also sad. She was amazed that Frau Klein was able to function at all. When Debbie, one of the little orphans back in Hope, had lost a kitten that she had found and was caring for, she had cried for days and refused to get out of bed. And even though Sara could see the sadness on her face, Frau Klein was bravely moving forward and getting back to her routine.

After Sara had finished eating, she got a stamp from Frau Klein, who refused to accept any money even when Sara tried to press some into her hand. Then she grabbed a light sweater and walked outside, hoping to find a mailbox to mail her letter. Peter had said that he would be back at the inn later that day, after doing some work for Dr. Pearlman. And Sara wanted to be there when he arrived. Even though she was still preoccupied with thinking about Frau Klein's situation, she needed to get back to focusing on the reason for her trip, and on what she was going to do next. So far every door had been closed in her face. Dr. Pearlman had made it clear that he wanted nothing to do with her, and the people who lived in what once was the DP camp had turned her away. She felt frustrated by her inability to uncover any information. Was she really going to be forced to abandon everything and catch the next flight home to Canada? No! She shook that thought away. She hadn't come all this way to turn back. There had to be something she could do. She just had to figure out what.

The sun shone brightly as she made her way through the streets of Wolfratshausen, turning this way and that, until she finally found what looked like a mailbox. Before dropping the letter inside, she stared at it in her hand and at the address for Loretta's Diner she had written on the front, hoping that Mrs. Clifford would find a way to get it to Dot. She wasn't sure if she'd hear back from her former roommate. And it didn't really matter one way or the other. Sara knew the letter was just her way of reaching out to someone who was important to her.

The sun beat down on her as she walked back to the inn, skipping over the puddles that dotted the sidewalk from the rain the day before. Cars honked as they drove past, and a flock of geese from the river called out in response. It felt good to be outside, and by the time she returned to the inn, she had worked up a sweat and had removed her sweater. Peter was already there, seated at the kitchen table and happily munching on a slice of poppy-seed cake that Frau Klein had just removed from the oven.

"You must think we don't do anything but eat here," he said when he saw her.

"I was beginning to wonder," Sara replied.

"We have an understanding here about Jewish mothers. They are a force of nature. They feed us, pamper us, protect us and often make us feel guilty. Frau Klein doesn't have any children, but she is definitely a Jewish mother!"

Sara laughed and sat down next to Peter. She was happy to see him. Frau Klein continued to hover around them, and Sara noticed that John Wayne's dishes had been removed from the floor while she had been out for her walk. She didn't say a word about it; she just stared at the empty space that had been John Wayne's spot. Her heart still ached for Frau Klein.

"Okay, what next?" Peter asked when he finally pushed his plate away and sat up to face Sara. "I assume you are not going to give up."

Sara cleared her head and quickly filled Peter in on the frustration she was feeling at not having been able to get any information about her mother.

"It's what I was trying to tell you," said Peter. "There aren't many people around here who want to talk about the past, or even admit that anything bad happened."

Sara paused. "I understand not wanting to remember. But surely they knew what was happening." Thinking back, even she had to admit that she was aware of Luke's harassing Malou back in Hope. She hadn't wanted to see what he was doing; she had wanted to mind her own business. But if she was being completely honest, she had to acknowledge that all the signs were there. She had chosen to ignore them. Sara knew from her reading that more than 150,000

German Jews had perished during the war. How did the citizens not see that? "What did everyone think when Jewish people were sent away?" she asked.

Peter leaned forward in his seat. "First of all, the cover story was that the concentration camps were a place to protect Jews from the discrimination that they were facing in their hometowns. People probably knew the camps existed, especially as the war went on. But I don't think they knew that Jews were being tortured and murdered there. The Nazis worked hard to keep that a secret."

"But what did everyone think when no one came back? They weren't living under a rock!" Peter looked confused, and Sara tried to explain. "You can only hide from the truth for so long," she said. "Eventually, you have to face what's happening in front of your eyes."

"Some people tried to help," Peter replied.

"But not enough."

Peter was trying to remain calm, but the discussion was heating him up. "There is no simple explanation here. Even if people did know about the camps, remember that there was not much that ordinary German civilians could have done without risking their own lives. People were scared. For themselves and for their families. It was safer to look the other way. That was also a reality."

"But—"

"Sara," Peter interrupted. "This is not a…how do you say it…a black-and-white situation. You're asking questions that perhaps we will never know the answers to."

He was right, of course, and Sara realized that it was wrong of her to put him on the spot like this—to try to have him explain or defend the activities of Germans during the war. But in reality, all of her questions boiled down to one simple one. How was she going to find out any information if people refused to talk about the past?

As she and Peter continued their conversation, Sara was aware of Frau Klein hovering close to them. The look on her face told Sara that she was desperately trying to understand what they were talking about, frowning every now and then and leaning forward to try to pick up a word or two. Suddenly, she began to talk to Peter in animated German. He responded while Sara slumped in her seat, wishing again that she could understand what they were saying. Every once in a while, she heard a word that sounded like "bad" coming from Frau Klein's lips. Is she talking about me? Sara wondered. Was Frau Klein also suggesting that Sara's plan to find someone to talk to was a terrible one? Without even realizing it, Sara began to rub her hands together, slowly at first and then with more intensity. This whole situation was making her feel sick.

Frau Klein turned and smiled at Sara, and then she walked out of the room.

"What was that all about?" Sara asked.

"It's just a suggestion," Peter began, "and it may be too hard or too crazy."

"Tell me!" Sara sat upright and leaned forward.

"Frau Klein knows of a place where the Germans have stored documents from the war. It's in a town north of here called Bad Arolsen."

"I heard Frau Klein saying the word *bad* and I thought she might have been talking about me."

Peter laughed softly. "Actually, *Bad* is the German word for spa. There is a center there, in Bad Arolsen, that has information—the names of Jews, which concentration camps they were sent to, and even how and when they died or were killed. The names of those who survived and went to the DP camps are also there."

"Let's go!" Sara leaped to her feet.

"Not so fast," replied Peter. "The town is about a four-hour train ride from here. It's a long trip. And even if you went there, I'm not sure they would let you in. The place has tight security, and not many people are allowed to enter."

Sara sank back down onto her chair. It was unfair to throw out a solution like this and then snatch it away from her because it was too difficult. Yes, she had to admit that there were obstacles in this proposal, but maybe the plan was doable. A four-hour train ride was not impossible, she thought. The fact that the place might not allow her in *was* a problem. But she would cross that bridge when she got there. The biggest hurdle of all was how she was going to communicate with the people who ran the center. But in her heart she knew this might be her shot to find out the truth about her mother—perhaps her only one. And she had to take it.

"Peter, I have to try this. Will you come with me?"

Peter looked into her eyes, perhaps a little too deeply. And then he replied, "Yes!"

Sixteen

SARA WAS IN Dr. Pearlman's office, seated on one of the couches in his waiting room. It was early—well before 6:00 AM. Peter had picked her up at Frau Klein's that morning but said he had to stop at the clinic first and put together a few things for the doctor. Sara was waiting for him to finish up. Their plan had developed quickly the day before. They hoped to catch the earliest train to Bad Arolsen, get to the center where the documents were stored, see what they could find and catch the last train back to Wolfratshausen. It would be a long and exhausting day but manageable—just as long as everything went according to plan. Sara stopped herself at that thought, refusing to dwell on the possibility that she might fail in her quest to find information about her mother. Today is the day that I will discover the truth, she told herself over and over.

She wasn't sure why she was so certain of this outcome. She just had to be.

The previous night, Sara had begun to dream about a real mother for the first time—her mother. She imagined a woman holding her in her arms, singing a lullaby and rocking her to sleep. The woman's face, though hazy, radiated kindness. Even in her dream, Sara knew that the image was far-fetched and implausible. And, of course, it had nothing to do with concentration camps or why Sara had been given up for adoption. That didn't matter. She had hunkered down in her sleep and hadn't wanted the fantasy to end.

The door to the clinic opened suddenly and Dr. Pearlman walked in. When he saw Sara, he stopped in his tracks, coughed into his hand and shut the door—just a little too loudly—behind him.

Calm down, Sara told herself. Don't overreact.

"Good morning," she said, keeping her voice even as she stood up. She was determined to be polite no matter what.

"Good morning," he muttered back, almost like he didn't want to respond but had no choice. He was just about to walk past her into the back room when he stopped and turned to face Sara.

"What are you doing here?" He was as gruff as he had been the last time they met—perhaps even more so.

"I'm—I'm just waiting for Peter." Oh why was she stuttering? Why was this man making her lose her confidence and her composure? She didn't even know him, and yet he was unnerving her so.

At that moment Peter appeared from the back. Dr. Pearlman glared at him and barked a brusque question in German. Peter glanced at Sara and then back at the doctor. Then he began to respond. Sara listened closely. She caught the words *Bad Arolsen* in their exchange and assumed that Peter was explaining where they were going.

"Why are you snooping around here so much?" Dr. Pearlman directed this question to Sara. "And why are you helping her?" This one was for Peter.

Peter was about to respond when Sara stepped in. "I don't have to tell you what my plans are. The last time I checked, this had become a free country."

"Don't be cheeky," Dr. Pearlman snapped. "You can't just appear out of nowhere and think you're going to get my assistance." The air was thick with his contempt.

"You've made it quite clear that you're not prepared to help me in any way."

"Please calm down, Herr Doktor," Peter interrupted. "We're leaving now and won't bother you with anything." He turned to escort Sara from the building, but she would not be stopped.

"Why do you care what I am doing?" she asked, shaking off Peter's arm. "And why are you so angry with me? I haven't done anything to you. I don't even know you, and yet you are doing everything in your power to make me feel like I'm an outsider—like I've done something wrong." This man was worse than the people living in what was once the DP camp. Those people had a reason for being so curt, as Peter had tried to explain. They were trying to erase the past and their possible roles in it. Why was this doctor trying to do the same? Had his past been so unbearable that he couldn't even be helpful to her? She could understand his pain at having lost his family. But that wasn't her fault. Why blame her as he seemed to be doing?

At any rate, Sara had had enough of his anger. And hers was starting to get the better of her. What she usually kept bottled inside rose in her throat and began to seep out against this horrible, mean man. Her hands found one another, but she forced them apart. She wasn't going to let her anxiety get the better of her—not now. She tossed her hair over her shoulder and faced the doctor. Her eyes flashed as she glared at him. "I don't have to answer any of your questions. If you're not prepared to help me, that's fine. But you can't stop me from trying to get my information."

They faced one another, separated by years of life experiences. Peter watched the exchange, not moving. Dr. Pearlman paused. His face trembled slightly, and his eyes glared back at Sara. As he reached up to rub his eyes, Sara could see the tattooed numbers on his arm. She refused to be unnerved by them.

"You're just..." he began.

Just what? Just getting in the way? Just being stubborn? Sara stood her ground in front of the doctor while Peter stood helplessly by. A moment later, the doctor turned and walked out the door.

Sara and Peter said little on the way to the train station. Even after they had purchased their tickets and boarded the train, and it had pulled away, she could still feel the fury of her exchange with the doctor. She was glad she had stood up to him. But her stomach was rolling up and down and from side to side even more than the train. And all the anger that had been directed at the doctor was now replaced with the more familiar apprehension. She hated the feeling!

She turned to stare out the window, trying to calm herself by watching the green, hilly land of the Bavarian south flatten as the train moved north toward the center of the country and their destination. Her breathing began to return to normal as she watched the countryside speed by. A full hour passed. Peter was the first to finally break the silence. He was sitting across from her, and he leaned forward to face her.

"I don't know what's gotten into Dr. Pearlman, but you have to trust me when I tell you that he isn't usually like this."

Sara wasn't sure she was ready to talk.

"You touched a nerve in him, that's for sure," Peter continued. "I don't think I've ever seen him this upset."

"Well, I guess he touched one in me too." She hesitated. "Mrs. Hazelton, the matron of the orphanage, once told me that I have a strong spirit. I think she used the word *fierce*."

"I can certainly vouch for that!" said Peter.

Sara smiled. "You know, I can't say that I was ever really happy growing up in the orphanage. Don't get me wrong," she added quickly. "Of course there were times when I felt good. It's just that, deep down, I never felt really content. But at least I knew what was what. Mrs. Hazelton was a wonderful matron, and my roommates were like sisters—*are* like sisters," she corrected herself before continuing. "I even had a boyfriend who I thought loved me." She didn't know why she was blurting all of this to Peter, but somehow she needed to get it out. She turned away from his stare. "Then, when the orphanage burned down, everything was turned upside down. It felt as if everything I knew in my life had been taken from me. I didn't know where I was going to live or what I was going to do."

"And the boyfriend?" Peter asked.

Sara smiled sadly. "He turned out to be nothing but trouble." She paused and took a breath. "But then Mrs. Hazelton gave me this information and told me that I had to figure out my past before I could figure out what I wanted to do with my life. I didn't think it would be this hard."

Peter continued to stare at her. "What do you want to do—with your life, I mean?"

"Well, maybe this sounds silly, but I've always loved to sew. One of my roommates, Dot, and I used to make clothes back in the orphanage. I've always dreamed of becoming a designer. But those are just dreams—wishful thinking."

"It's not silly at all. And dreams are important," Peter said. "My parents are always telling me to think big and then find a way to catch up with the ideas."

Sara smiled. "I like that." No one had ever paid much attention to what she desired for her future.

Luke had just laughed when she talked about wanting to design clothes.

"You can find a way to make that one happen," Peter continued. "I'm sure of it."

Sara felt her face redden, and she quickly tried to shift the conversation. "What about you?" she asked. "Do you think about what you want to do one day?"

Peter didn't hesitate. "Medicine. Despite what you've seen of Dr. Pearlman, I've admired his skills for years. That's why I've worked for him at the clinic. I've watched him—the way he attends to his patients, the way he figures out what's wrong with them and then finds a solution. I'm going to be a doctor."

"I think you'll make a good one," Sara said.

Peter finally broke the awkward silence that followed. "It's unusual for Jewish girls to have such blue eyes."

Sara laughed out loud. "I wish I knew where they came from," she said. "It's all part of what I'm trying to discover. I have no idea what my parents looked like."

"I've always been told that I look like my father." Peter had short reddish-brown hair and dark-brown eyes. "Most of the Jewish people around here look like me—dark hair, dark eyes. It was usually the Aryans who were blond-haired and had blue eyes, like you."

Sara looked puzzled. "Aryans?" she asked. There was something familiar about that word from the reading she had done, but she couldn't place it.

"Another term from the past," replied Peter. "It's simply a racial grouping. But Adolf Hitler believed that Aryans were what he called the master race—the most superior of all. Jews were not part of that desirable group and were mistreated for their religion, culture, background and, yes, even for their appearance."

It was still unimaginable to Sara that such attitudes had once existed.

"I like them." Peter was still talking. "Your blue eyes, I mean."

Sara blushed again. Just then the train listed to one side, and Peter was thrown forward, bringing his face practically up against hers. He steadied himself but stayed there a moment longer—his face close to hers. She could almost feel his breath against her skin and could see his mouth just inches from hers. A moment later, he moved back into his seat. They didn't talk again until the train pulled into the Bad Arolsen station.

Seventeen

SARA AND PETER stood facing the International Tracing Service building in the middle of Bad Arolsen. It was a solid and impressive-looking brick building encircled by an iron fence. The fence was intimidating enough. The added problem was the security men who stood guard in front, one at the gate and another farther down the walkway, at the front door of the building. The men wore uniforms, though neither Peter nor Sara could identify what they were. German police? Private security? International inspectors? It didn't matter. The men were there to keep visitors like Sara out.

"Why does it look so much like a prison?" Sara asked.

Peter began to explain. "Under Adolf Hitler, the Nazis kept detailed records about their own activities—who they rounded up and killed, where it happened and how. All of that information has been brought here. But I guess this country is not yet ready for the world to see any of it. So they keep it locked up—tightly!"

The two of them continued to stare at the guards.

"What do you think we should do?" Peter finally asked.

Sara had been hatching a plan and decided that now was the time to put it into action. She turned to Peter. "Put your arm around my waist and follow my lead," she directed. Peter was taken aback and looked confused. "Don't ask any questions," she said. "Just follow me."

With only the briefest hesitation, Peter hooked his arm around Sara's waist, and together they began to move toward the iron gate and the first guard. As they drew closer, Sara suddenly slumped against Peter's body and hung her head on his shoulder.

"Halt!" the guard ordered as they approached. The man had a thick neck, and his hands were folded across a uniform that stretched across an overly ample belly. His head was the shape of a full moon, and his jaw jutted out as if someone were pulling on the bottom half of his face.

"Please," Sara gasped. "I need to use the bathroom!" She doubled over, coughing and pretending to retch into her hand.

"*Das ist verboten!*" The guard took a menacing step toward Sara.

She could make out a word that sounded like "forbidden" in what he had just growled at them. "I'm going to throw up," she tried again, grabbing her stomach and contorting her face.

That's when Peter took up the script. "You've got to let us in," he pleaded. "She's going to be sick right here."

As if to prove his point, Sara coughed again, gagging violently. The guard hesitated. Sara coughed louder, lifting her face directly into his.

"Please," Peter begged. "Before it's too late."

At that, the guard stepped back and quickly moved to open the gate. He grabbed his walkie-talkie to signal to his colleague at the front door of the building. Peter and Sara picked up their pace, lurching through the set of gates, up to the front door and past the second, startled security guard who had opened it and stood aside.

"Toilet?" Peter asked.

The guard at the front door pointed down the hallway and stood back, covering his own mouth with a handkerchief as Sara heaved once more.

"That was brilliant," Peter said once they had turned a corner. He held his arm around her waist for a moment longer, until Sara moved away from him and smiled.

"I've lived in an orphanage all my life. You'd be surprised at how many ways there are to get around doing chores or get out of trouble." This had been almost too simple. "You were pretty good yourself," she added.

"Just following your lead," he replied. "But what do we do if we run into another guard?"

Sara took a deep breath. "One obstacle at a time."

The two of them surveyed the signs that dotted the hallway. They were written in German and meant nothing to Sara, but Peter investigated them closely. "There," he said, pointing to one of the arrows. "I think the records of those who were in the DP camps will be in that room." He indicated a door that was just meters from where they stood.

Through the square glass pane, they could see a middle-aged woman seated at a desk in front of a stack of files and papers. Her short dark hair was brushed neatly behind her ears, and her glasses were perched precariously on the end of her nose as she worked over her files.

Once more, Peter turned to Sara. "You're the one who seems to know how to get around these obstacles. Any ideas?"

Sara surveyed the situation and then made a decision. Enough pretending, she thought. It was time to take her chances on being completely honest. She grabbed Peter by the arm, and together they opened the door of the records room and walked inside.

The woman behind the desk looked up, startled, as the two young people entered her office. "*Was machen Sie hier*?" She stood quickly, nearly losing the glasses off her nose. Sara did not need an interpreter to understand that the woman was asking what they were doing there. The rectangular nameplate at the front of her desk was engraved with the name Hedda Kaufmann.

Peter began to respond, but Sara reached out and put her hand on his arm. "Let me," she said and turned to the woman. "Do you speak English?" she asked.

The startled woman nodded. "Yes, of course. Who are you, and how did you get in here? Where are the security guards?" She reached for the telephone on her desk, but Sara placed her hand on top of the woman's.

"Before you call anyone, please let me tell you what this is all about."

She began to talk, explaining that she had lived in an orphanage in Canada up until the day that a fire had burned her home to the ground. She described Mrs. Hazelton and the other six girls, and the journeys that each of them was taking to find out who they were and where they had come from. Finally, she talked about the discovery that her mother was Jewish, had survived a concentration camp and had given birth to her in the Föhrenwald displaced persons camp. The woman remained standing throughout Sara's speech. Her face was expressionless, and Sara had no idea what she was thinking. "I'm staying at the Landhaus Inn in Wolfratshausen—with Frau Klein. I have less than a week to find information about my mother and father—who they were and what happened to them. Please don't turn me away." Sara glanced at the nameplate on the desk. "Frau Kaufmann?" Her voice was pleading. "You're pretty much my last hope."

With that, she stood silently in front of the woman. Seconds passed while Hedda Kaufmann eyed Sara up and down. Sara could almost see the debate going on inside the woman's head while she pondered what Sara had said and decided whether to help. Finally, she gestured toward Peter. "And who is this young man? Is he searching for someone too?"

Sara let out the breath she had been holding. She detected that the harshness had gone out of Frau Kaufmann's voice. "Peter is my friend. He's been helping me."

Frau Kaufmann hesitated. "I shouldn't be doing this..." she said, while Sara stood facing her, hope and expectation written across her face. "All right," the woman finally said, moving out from behind her desk. "Come with me."

Eighteen

SARA'S HEART WAS jumping, her pulse racing. She could barely contain her excitement as she and Peter followed Frau Kaufmann into a back room. Metal filing cabinets filled the space, lined up side by side to create a maze of narrow passageways. Frau Kaufmann walked up and down the aisles, checking the nameplates on several of the cabinets, searching for something. Sara didn't know what. Finally, Frau Kaufmann came to a stop in front of a row of filing cabinets at the back of the room. "Ah, here they are." She turned to face Peter and Sara, who had followed silently behind her. "The records of those who were in Föhrenwald are here in these cabinets." She glanced down the aisle, to the door leading back to her front office. "You have about twenty minutes. I can't allow you any more time than that." And with that she turned and walked away.

Sara wasted no time. She surveyed the cabinet drawers, searching for the nameplate with the letters closest to her mother's last name—Frankel. It did not take long for her to find the right one. She pulled the drawer open, flipped through the records contained inside and finally withdrew a single slim file folder. The label read *Frankel, Karen.* Glancing at Peter, Sara moved to a small table next to the cabinets. She sat down and steadied herself. Here it was. Her journey had led her to this place, this moment, and to the information she was about to uncover inside these pages. Why the hesitation in opening the file? she asked herself. What was she going to find? And how would it change her life or her future?

"Are you going to open it or just stare at it?" Peter asked.

Sara laughed nervously. "I'm suddenly so scared," she replied.

Peter took a step closer to the table and placed his hand on Sara's shoulder. "Open it," he said. "It's what you've come for."

Sara nodded, exhaled loudly and flipped open the file. There was hardly anything inside, just a couple of documents and letters with a bit of information about the brief life of Karen Frankel.

"There's so little here," said Sara, shaking her head.

"I can't imagine someone's life reduced to a few sheets of paper." Peter was peering over Sara's shoulder at the information.

Everything had gone a little blurry in front of Sara's eyes. Yes, her mother's whole life was here in this thin file. But then again, Sara's life had also been reduced to two documents and a gold necklace. She fingered the Star of David around her neck as her vision came back into focus. "Peter, you have to read this for me."

Peter nodded and exchanged places with Sara. He began to read aloud, translating as he went. "It says here that your mother was imprisoned in the Auschwitz concentration camp. It says that she was there for six months."

"I can't even imagine what her life must have been like there," Sara interrupted. She knew that Jewish prisoners were starved, tortured and killed in that awful place. She shook her head, trying to push the images away, and turned back to Peter. "Keep going."

"She went to Föhrenwald in June 1945, just after Auschwitz was liberated by the Soviet army."

"She must have been pregnant with me when she arrived." Sara was doing a quick mental calculation. The medical certificate that she had, signed by Dr. Pearlman, said that she had been born in

December 1945, six months after her mother arrived in Föhrenwald. "What about my father? Is there anything in there about him?"

Peter flipped to another sheet of paper. He scanned the document and then lifted his face to Sara. "I found his name. Simon Frankel."

The information was right in front of Sara. Her father and her mother—Simon and Karen Frankel.

"They married just months before their deportation together to Auschwitz. It appears that they had survived up until that time with false papers that identified them as Christians." Peter looked up. "Most German Jews were deported to the concentration camps early on in the war. It's pretty miraculous that your parents were able to hide for so long."

"It didn't do them much good in the end," Sara said bitterly.

Peter returned to the document. "It says here that your father survived in Auschwitz for the first few months after they arrived. They were separated from each other, but both were alive. And then..." Peter paused. "He was killed a few months later. Your father died in the gas chambers." These last words were said in barely more than a whisper.

Sara cleared her throat. "I figured that much. Even though my mother survived until the end of the war, I know that she was really sick by then—with tuberculosis—TB. I contracted it from her." She stared at Peter.

"It doesn't say anything about you in here."

"I can only imagine that my mother tried to hide her pregnancy while she was in the concentration camp. Is there anything else?" asked Sara.

Peter continued reading and then stopped.

"What is it?"

"It says that eventually your mother was transported for treatment to a hospital in Gauting—about ten miles from Föhrenwald. She died there."

Neither one of them spoke. So there it was—the answer to Sara's questions about her background. Her parents were both dead. Not that she was really surprised to learn that; it was what she had expected, despite the shards of hope that had slipped in and out of her imagination. Yet strangely, even though all the information had just been confirmed, Sara did not feel resolved about her past. She just felt sad.

"I'm sorry," Peter began.

Sara shook her head. "At least I know what happened, and why I was given up for adoption. There was no one to take care of me after both of them died. I guess I'm lucky that Dr. Pearlman cleared the way for me to go to Canada." She began to gather the papers back into the file. Just as she was about to replace it in the cabinet, a single black-and-white photograph slipped out from between the sheets and fell to the ground. Sara bent to pick it up. There was a young girl standing in the picture. Her long curly hair was held off her face with two clips. She was straddling a bicycle and staring, without smiling, into the camera. Sara knew instantly that this was her mother—a reflection of her own face was gazing back at her. She was staring at the photo when Hedda Kaufmann re-entered the file room.

"I'm afraid it's time," Frau Kaufmann said. "I've allowed you to stay in here for as long as possible." She saw Sara staring at the photograph and approached her. As she peered over Sara's shoulder, Frau Kaufmann gasped out loud. "Karen!" she said.

"What?" Sara, startled out of her sadness, looked up at Frau Kaufmann.

"It's Karen Frankel. Is she the one you were looking for? Was she your mother?"

"Did you know her?"

"Yes, she was my friend," replied Frau Kaufmann, reaching for the photo and holding it tenderly in her hands. "We were in the same barrack in Auschwitz and then together again in Föhrenwald. I'm also a survivor of the Holocaust. I had no idea that you were looking for Karen."

They stared at one another, Frau Kaufmann taking in Sara's long dark hair and piercing blue eyes.

And then she gasped again. "Of course, you must be the child!"

"Please," begged Sara, "you have to tell me what you know about my mother. What was she like? Was she kind? Was she funny?" It felt to her as if she had suddenly been thrown a lifeline—the opportunity to learn some details about her mother that might connect her to Sara's life in a meaningful way—not just facts documented in a file, but real and personal information.

Frau Kaufmann stuttered and stammered and looked away.

Sara was confused by her reaction. "Is something wrong?"

"It's too terrible," Frau Kaufmann replied. "I can't possibly tell you."

"Tell me what?"

"The guards, they treated us so badly there. So many of us were beaten and tortured."

"Yes, I can't even begin to imagine how you must have suffered. But is there something that you know about my mother?" Sara felt that recognizable dread rise up in her like an unwanted visitor.

"One guard in particular," Frau Kaufmann continued, breathless now and with eyes closed. "He had it in for the young women. He singled out your mother. She had no way to fend him off."

A belt was beginning to tighten around Sara's chest, crushing the air out of her lungs. She fought to breath, forcing air into her lungs. "What are you trying to say?"

"But perhaps killing her would have been better than..."

"Than what?"

"It's too terrible," Frau Kaufmann whispered again.

"Stop saying that, Frau Kaufmann! Please! You've got to tell me what it is!" Sara gulped. "It's about my mother. It's about my life."

The room felt as if it had gone icy cold, like a winter day back in Hope. The hairs on Sara's arms stood straight up as she faced Frau Kaufmann, impatient yet fearful of what was coming next. And then, finally, Frau Kaufmann spoke. Sara had to lean in to hear what she said.

"There is no other way to tell you this except to be honest with you. Your mother was raped in the final days of the war. The man who raped her was the Nazi concentration-camp guard. She was pregnant with you when she arrived in Föhrenwald."

Nineteen

PETER WAS MOUTHING something, but the thumping in Sara's chest had risen up to her ears, pounding and drowning out all other sounds. Peter, Frau Kaufmann, the records room—all of it fell away. A voice screamed inside Sara's head—perhaps she even screamed it aloud—"No, no, no!" And then Sara fled from the room. She could hear Frau Kaufmann behind her, calling out to her.

"Wait! Please stop! You mustn't leave like this."

Sara ignored her cries. She ran down the hallway of the building, out the front door and toward the front gates, where the beefy guard was still standing. Tears streamed down her cheeks. Her heart was beating so wildly that she had to place her hands on either side of her chest, as if to keep it from breaking through her ribs. The guard took one look at her and rushed to unlock the gates. This time, Sara thought she might really be sick.

Her mind was in overdrive. The last words from Frau Kaufmann's mouth rewound through her brain like a broken record. *The man who raped your mother was the Nazi concentration-camp guard.* How was that possible? How was it that she had traveled all this way to find out about her family only to discover that her father—her *father*—was a Nazi guard? What did that even mean? Was she also part Nazi? And what part had come from him? The anger? The irritation? The blue eyes? It was almost too much to imagine.

Sara ran toward the train station. The tears were streaming from her eyes so hard and fast that she could barely see where she was going. Her hands were clasped and grinding furiously against one another as if she could somehow erase the moment if she rubbed hard enough. Everything was coming apart. It was like pulling a thread on the hem of a skirt that she had sewn and watching as it unraveled.

Somehow one foot found its way in front of the other, and miraculously Sara made it to the train station. But what now? There were no trains in sight. And even if there had been one, she had no idea where she wanted to be. Wolfratshausen? Hope? Neither was a good option at that moment. Sara was dizzy, and she closed her eyes while the earth spun around her. And finally, with no other alternative, she slumped on a bench, and only then did she bury her head in her hands as sobs rippled through her body. Minutes passed, and she became aware of someone standing next to her. When she finally peeled her hands away from her eyes, she saw Peter hovering above her.

"Are you okay?" His face was creased with worry.

She squeezed her eyes shut, trying to obliterate the realization of what had just happened. It would have been better if she could have just disappeared into the ground. "No, I'm not okay."

Peter did not reply. He shifted from one foot to the other, waiting awkwardly, fidgeting as if he was trying to decide what to do.

"It all makes perfect sense now," Sara finally gasped between sobs. "That's why my mother gave me away. It's not just that there was no one to look after me. My mother hated me. How could she not hate me after what happened to her, after realizing who...what...that man was..." She couldn't even say the word *father* anymore.

"But none of this was your fault. You were just a baby."

"It doesn't matter. Every time she looked at me, she must have seen him. That would have been enough to make her want to get rid of me."

Another long moment of silence passed.

"Why did I even come here?" Sara finally moaned. "Mrs. Hazelton said I had to figure out the past. But she was so wrong. What good could any of this do me?" There was no moving forward in her life, Sara thought. She was tethered to her past like a horse to a cart. She could no more escape it than she could sprout wings and fly. "I wish I had never known about my mother," Sara cried. "I wish I had never come to Germany."

The train pulled into the station, and Peter and Sara climbed on board. They rode the long journey back to Wolfratshausen in painful silence.

Sara fled to her room when she arrived back at Frau Klein's inn, but not before she had run her hands under cool water to ease the burn from having rubbed them raw. Then she threw herself onto her bed, burying her head in her pillow. She wanted to cry; she wanted to scream. But there was no fight, no tears, no feeling, left inside of her. She was simply numb. Finally, she rolled over onto her side, staring at the copy of *The Diary of Anne Frank* on her bedside table as if Anne could somehow provide some answers for her, all the time knowing that there were no solutions here.

Then she glanced out the window. The baby robins had been growing steadily and quickly over the previous few days, and one by one they were beginning to fly from the nest. Three were already gone, and Sara could make out the mother robin perched in a tree close by, chirping madly to try to convince the last baby to leave. But it had hunkered down and did not appear to want to go anywhere. "Better to stay put for as long as you can," Sara whispered to the last baby bird. "The world can be a horrible place."

With that, Sara fell into a fitful sleep and began to dream. It started with everything dark and cloudy around her. Smoke filled her lungs, making it difficult to breathe. Was this the fire that had consumed the orphanage? Where was Mrs. Hazelton? And where had her roommates gone? Were they safe? Sara strained to make out something familiar in the murky surroundings. And then slowly the fog began to lift, and she realized that she was not back in Hope. She found herself standing on the precipice of an empty grave. Faceless men and women surrounded her, some dressed in prison garb, others in the uniforms of Nazi guards. Everyone was shuffling forward and pushing Sara toward the edge of the pit. At first she resisted and fought back against the surge. But then one of the guards raised a gun, and a single pistol shot rang out by her head. Sara was thrown forward into the air, and she found herself falling, falling, falling into the blackness below. She hit the dirt at the bottom and rolled over to look up. The guard who had shot her was standing above her at the edge of the pit, sneering down at her. It was the face of a monster, massive and menacing. But when Sara looked closer, she was horrified to realize that the face staring down into the grave was hers. She had become the Nazi guard!

She awoke in a sweat and bolted upright, breathing heavily and searching the room for something familiar to ground her back in reality. She had only been asleep for a few minutes, but it had felt like an eternity. Sara lay her head back down on the pillow and tried to control the wild beating of her heart while pushing the grisly images of her nightmare somewhere far away. It took several minutes for her breathing to return to normal.

What was she going to do now? It was the question that reverberated through her brain, pounding like a sledgehammer. With a couple of days left before she was due to fly home, perhaps she should just go to the airport and try to get an earlier flight. There was nothing left to discover here. To stay or to go? Sara, who had been so good at making decisions for herself on this journey, suddenly felt completely immobilized. She needed help with this decision. But who to turn to? There was only one person she could think of.

She wandered downstairs, looking for Frau Klein, and found her where else but in the kitchen, preparing dinner. Frau Klein could not hide the worry in her eyes. Peter had likely told her what had happened in Bad Arolsen. But in this moment it was probably a good thing that Sara and Frau Klein couldn't communicate. Sara wasn't in the mood for a conversation. So she settled for Frau Klein's sympathetic glances and the tender hand she placed on Sara's arm. She knew that Frau Klein was still dealing with her own loss of John Wayne. And even though she did not want to talk, she appreciated the gesture and smiled gratefully at the innkeeper. Then she accepted a tray of food and indicated that she needed to use the telephone. Frau Klein nodded vigorously and pointed her toward the office at the back of the inn, where a telephone sat on a small desk in one corner.

Sara walked into the back room and sank down into the chair in front of the desk. It was adorned with pictures of John Wayne, from the time he was a young pup right up until shortly before Sara had met him several days earlier. It was a small shrine to the animal that had been Frau Klein's companion, and Sara gulped hard before picking up the telephone receiver. The line crackled and came alive with a woman's voice.

"*Guten Tag, wer spricht da?*"

It had to be the operator. "Oh, I do hope you speak English," Sara began, speaking slowly and clearly. "I need to place a long-distance telephone call to Canada." She went on to give the telephone number of the nursing home where Mrs. Hazelton had been staying.

"One moment, please," the operator replied, while Sara gave silent thanks for having been understood. Several minutes later, another female voice came on the line.

"Cartwright Nursing Home. Mrs. Luxton speaking. How can I help you?"

Sara's heart leaped. "Yes, hello," she replied. "I'd like to speak to Mrs. Hazelton. She's a patient there."

There was a long pause. "Agnes Hazelton?"

It was always hard to think of the matron by her first name. "Yes, that's correct. I'd like to speak to her, please."

"I'm sorry. Agnes Hazelton has been discharged."

Sara felt her hopes plummet. "Oh, well, can you tell me where she's gone?"

"I'm sorry. We are unable to give out that information."

Sara tried again. "Mrs. Luxton, is it? I used to live at the orphanage where Mrs. Hazelton was the matron. I'm sure she wouldn't mind if you told me where—"

"I'm sorry," Mrs. Luxton interrupted. "That is privileged information that I am not permitted to divulge."

"But you see I'm calling long distance. From Germany." The line was beginning to crackle again and fade. "Hello? Can you hear me?"

A moment later, the phone went dead in Sara's hand. She was completely alone again.

Dejected, Sara headed back to the kitchen. On the way, she passed a room with its door partly open. She didn't know what drew her closer to have a look. But with hardly a thought, Sara approached the door and pushed it open. She poked her head inside and was startled to see a sewing machine in one corner of the room and piles of fabric lying off to the side. It was as if she had re-entered the common room of the Benevolent Home back in Hope, and for a moment Sara was transported back in time to that place where she and Dot had shared many long nights, dreaming of their future careers and dancing on the open floor. At another time, Sara would have been overjoyed to see this space. But in that moment, she was almost too numbed by her circumstances to feel anything. It was there that Frau Klein found her a few minutes later.

"Oh, I'm so sorry," Sara said when Frau Klein entered the room. "I was just snooping around. I shouldn't be in here." Even though she knew that

Frau Klein couldn't possibly understand her apology, Sara felt compelled to explain herself.

She started to leave the room, but Frau Klein placed a hand on her arm and said something in German. The innkeeper gestured around the room and dragged Sara over to the piles of fabric, pulling a bundle from the top and placing it in Sara's hands. Then she practically pushed her down onto the chair in front of the sewing machine. Sara didn't have to understand a word to know that Frau Klein was telling her she was welcome in this room. Sara reached over to give the innkeeper a warm hug. They were leaving the room arm in arm when Peter entered the inn.

"I was so worried about you," he said after greeting Frau Klein. "Are you all right?"

Sara shrugged. "I've been better."

"Would you like to go outside? It's a perfect night," he said. "Let's get some air."

Sara and Peter walked out of the inn and into the garden at the back. Rows of red, yellow and purple flowers encircled the yard, crowding together like visitors at a tourist attraction. Bees happily buzzed around the blooms. The sun was low on the horizon. The sky was clear. And stars were just beginning to peek out. It was, as Peter had said, a beautiful night. He steered Sara to a wooden garden swing that sat off to one side. They sat down side by side under the canvas canopy.

At first there was little to say. Sara was still wrapped up in the discovery of the circumstances of her birth, and Peter was also struggling.

"I don't know what to say to you," he finally said. "I'm trying to find the right words, but I don't know how to be helpful."

"There's nothing to say," Sara replied. "And there's no way that you can help. Everything is a disaster right now."

More silence followed.

"I tried to call the matron of my orphanage," Sara finally continued. "But even she wasn't there."

"What do you think she would have said if you had reached her?"

Sara thought for a moment. It was a good question. "Oh, she would have said that I need to be strong. She would have said that there is a reason for everything. And she would have told me that I need to learn from this moment and move forward."

"She sounds like a very wise person," Peter replied.

"But that's so much easier said than done," cried Sara. "The man who raped my mother was a Nazi. That means that part of him is in me as well. Do you understand that? I was a mistake from the beginning.

A horrible, horrible mistake. How do I ever move on from that?"

Peter paused before replying. "From everything that I know and can see of you, there is no Nazi sitting in front of me. You are not that."

It was small comfort.

"What are you going to do now?" Peter asked.

Dejected, Sara replied, "I think I need to go back to Hope."

"And what will you do there?" Peter's voice was small and sad.

Sara shook her head. She had no answer.

"Don't go, Sara," Peter begged, turning to face her. "Stay here. Perhaps there is more that you can find. You've only been here a few days."

Sara shook her head sadly. "There's nothing for me here. I was never wanted—not by my mother, not by anyone."

Peter moved closer, until his face was just inches from hers. Electricity passed through Sara's body as the hairs on Peter's arm brushed against hers. "Don't go," he repeated.

In Sara's mind there was a fleeting memory of Luke having begged her to stay with him back in Hope—the same plea but different in every possible way.

And then Peter took her in his arms and kissed her. His lips pressed against hers, softly at first and then with more strength. Sara hesitated for a moment and then wrapped her arms around Peter's neck and allowed him to pull her close. There had been other first kisses in her life—with Luke and once before that with a boy in one of her classes. Those kisses had been interesting and even exciting. But this kiss was like no other. It was the tenderness of it that took Sara's breath away. And this time, the anxiety that pumped through her body was intertwined with longing and passion and gratitude and a bundle of other emotions that were hard to figure out.

"Please stay," Peter whispered in her ear. "I want you here."

Sara pulled herself away from Peter's embrace, looked into his eyes and replied, "I can't."

Twenty

EARLY THE NEXT morning, Peter arrived at Frau Klein's inn to pick up Sara and walk her over to Dr. Pearlman's office. She would wait for him to finish up some work, and then he was going to accompany her to a travel agent Frau Klein had suggested, who would change her flight to Canada. She and Peter had said nothing to one another about the previous evening's kiss. There was an awkwardness between them. Sara didn't like it. She had felt so comfortable, so at ease with him. This strain was unfamiliar and distressing. She longed for the relationship to return to what it had been before, but she didn't know how to get it there. And she was also confused by the feelings that were bubbling up inside of her. There was no hiding the fact that she was attracted to Peter. He had awoken a desire in her that she had tried to push away. A relationship with him is a terrible idea, she told herself. She was returning to Canada, and he was living in Germany. That alone was an insurmountable obstacle. And after discovering her origins, Sara wasn't sure she was worthy of a relationship with anyone. It would probably turn into a mess, just like everything else in her life. Perhaps it was better to say goodbye to Peter before anything started. And yet...somehow that didn't feel right either.

As she sat in Dr. Pearlman's waiting room, Sara tried to calm her nerves and fight the fatigue that was threatening to overtake her. The previous night's sleep had been fitful again. Every time she closed her eyes, the recurring nightmare had begun—Sara on the edge of a pit, her face that of a Nazi guard. In the end, she had been afraid to fall asleep. As she sat trying to breathe deeply, she also tried to keep herself from rubbing her hands together. It wasn't easy, and in the end she simply clasped them tightly in her lap and waited impatiently for Peter to finish his work.

The bell above the door chimed, and when Sara looked up, Dr. Pearlman was standing at the entrance. He paused, slightly startled to see her, and then began to walk past without saying a word. Sara couldn't resist speaking up.

"You'll be happy to know that you got what you wanted." The doctor paused but didn't turn around. "I'm leaving," she continued. "You never have to see me again." This time he turned slowly and stared long and hard at Sara. "You were right," she added, thrusting her chin into the air. "There is nothing for me here. And snooping around did nothing except bring me information I didn't want to know."

Dr. Pearlman nodded. And then, with a slight hesitation, he approached her. "What did you...find out?" he asked, faltering a bit and then regaining his composure.

"I'm not sure why you're interested, but I found out that the only reason I was born is that my mother was raped in the concentration camp." Sara said it defiantly, angrily. She wasn't sure why she had hurled out this news to the person who had pushed her away so harshly. Perhaps she was punishing herself by blurting the information to Dr. Pearlman. Perhaps she expected the doctor to say something like, *I told you so. That'll teach you to go meddling where you shouldn't.* And she would have agreed. But, surprisingly, he didn't say a word. His eyes even appeared to have softened.

"My mother must have thought I was a monster," Sara continued bitterly. "Just like the man who hurt her."

Silence hung in the air between them. Dr. Pearlman appeared to be struggling—wanting to say something and then stopping himself. He opened his mouth, hesitated, shut it, then opened it again. And then, finally, he began to speak. "You were no monster," he said softly. "You were an innocent baby—a beautiful, innocent baby."

Sara frowned. What was he saying?

"You were terribly sick as an infant—a frail baby bird. And Karen was so sick when she gave birth to you."

Karen? Why was he calling her mother by her first name?

"We were all afraid to look at you, knowing where and how you had been conceived. But not Karen. She held you in her arms and the look in her eyes as she gazed at you was pure love."

Peter entered the room, and Sara put her finger to her lips to tell him to be quiet. Dr. Pearlman was talking as if he were the only one in the room, oblivious to Sara and Peter. Sara did not want to interrupt his flow of words: he had just said that her mother had loved her.

"Those first few days after she was hospitalized, she wouldn't let you go. She held on to you as if together you could give each other strength to heal. Even as she grew weaker and we tried to pry you from her arms, she still refused to let you go. And then she finally took her last breath and she was gone."

Sara couldn't contain herself. She rose from the couch. "Dr. Pearlman, what are you saying? Were you there when I was born? Were you there when my mother died?" Sara had thought he'd simply signed the medical document to allow her to go to Canada. But there was so much more that he was implying here.

"You can't possibly understand how much I'd lost in the camps—how much we all suffered," he continued, refusing to meet Sara's eyes. His voice dropped, and Sara strained to hear what he would say next.

"Do you know how the Nazis killed some Jews in the camps? Yes, you know about the gas chambers. But that was only one way that they demonstrated their cruelty. One day they lined the women up in twos, facing one another. My beautiful wife was among them. Then they went down the line, firing one bullet into the head of the first of each pair. One bullet that entered the brain of the first woman and then traveled into and through the brain of the second. One bullet for two women. They could save ammunition that way. Effective, no? Economical! Only the Nazis could think of something so evil." He spat these last words out as if he couldn't bear to say them.

Sara did not move. Her hand was at her mouth. She didn't want to hear more details of how the doctor's wife had been killed. It was painful to hear Dr. Pearlman describe this horrific scene. And yet she sensed that there was more he had to say—and more that she needed to know.

"They were all gone. My beautiful wife, dead in the camps, and my beautiful Karen, dead in the hospital. And the only one left was you, her baby... my grandchild." And with this last declaration, Dr. Pearlman finally raised his eyes and stared at Sara.

The room began to spin around her, and Sara reached out for the couch to steady herself. "That's not possible," she finally sputtered. "Are you saying that you were her father? That you were...are...my grandfather?"

He nodded. "Yes."

Her grandfather! This should have been a joyful moment, her discovering that she had a grandfather who was alive. But there was no joy inside of her. Instead, Sara could feel an electrical current spreading from her toes to her stomach and settling there like an angry hot ember.

"Then you're the one who gave me away! Not my mother. It was you."

Dr. Pearlman nodded again and whispered, "Yes."

She was burning up from the inside out—an inferno like the fire that had devastated the orphanage in Hope. She too felt destroyed.

"But how could you do that? How could you abandon me knowing that even my mother had forgiven me for being conceived that way? You said that she loved me. Why couldn't you do the same?"

Dr. Pearlman's face crumpled, and she thought he might fall to the ground. And despite the rage that burned inside of her, she reached out to steady him. The doctor clasped her hand and held it tightly.

"Please try to understand," he begged. "There was no way on earth that I could care for you then. And I was so worried that you would be stained by the circumstances of your birth. Your blue eyes—they announced to everyone who your real father was. I couldn't bear for you to suffer that scrutiny or judgment. So I did the only thing I could think of to give you a chance at a normal life. I gave you up for adoption." Sara tried to pull free of his grasp, but he held her even tighter. "I couldn't save my wife or my daughter. But I hoped, by sending you away, that somehow I could help you. Sometimes you have to abandon someone in order to save them."

Sara was not satisfied with that. "Why didn't you tell me any of this?" she cried. "Why did you turn on me when I came in here?"

The doctor finally released her hand. He closed his eyes before speaking again. "I knew I was doing the right thing to give you up. But it has not been easy for me. I've lived with the guilt of not having kept you for all these years. When you walked in here a few days ago and I realized who you were, I simply couldn't face you. And so I lashed out instead. I'm so very sorry," he added, opening his eyes to stare at Sara. "For everything."

It was Sara's turn to squeeze her eyes shut. She was exhausted. This was all simply too much for her to hear and understand. Her anger, her fear, her anxiety—all were seeping out of her body, leaving her numb. She opened her eyes to stare at Dr. Pearlman. He suddenly seemed old and fragile, and in that moment it was Sara who yearned to reach out to comfort him. She took a step toward the doctor and placed her hand on his shoulder. And then he grabbed her, wrapped his arms around her and buried his face in her shoulder. His sobs echoed in the room as they stood together, not moving.

Minutes passed, and then Peter cleared his throat behind Sara. She had almost forgotten that he was there. Dr. Pearlman released her and took a step back, fumbling in his pocket for a handkerchief to wipe his eyes.

"I want you to know that Simon Frankel loved your mother deeply—they loved each other. He is the man who should have been your father."

Sara nodded. It was a bit of comfort. "What happened to her? My mother. I mean, I know that she died, but is there a cemetery around here where she's buried?"

"Yes," the doctor replied. "She's buried in the Jewish cemetery close to Gauting—the hospital she was taken to from Föhrenwald. I haven't been there since her death. I can't bear to go. You are like your mother in so many ways," he added. "She was spirited and as determined as you."

Peter finally moved over to stand next to Sara, taking her arm as if to lead her from the building. But Sara wasn't sure that Dr. Pearlman had finished. And she was right.

"Your name—Sara," he said. "It's a Jewish tradition to name a child after a family member who has died. You are named after my late wife—your grandmother. Karen, I mean your mother, wanted you to have that name."

Each puzzle piece was finally clicking into place, and Sara was feeling as if she could finally breathe again.

"There's one final thing," added Dr. Pearlman. "The Star of David that you wear around your neck. It was your mother's. It was the one thing she managed to save, even in the concentration camp. To this day, I don't know how she kept it. I removed it from her neck after she died and placed it around yours. The letters on it—they spell out the Hebrew word *tikvah*. It means 'hope.'"

Sara gasped. Her hands flew to her neck and to the necklace. It was the ultimate irony that Hope, the town in which she had been raised, the place that had always meant so little to her, was the final message her mother had left her. Peter placed his arm around her shoulder and squeezed it slightly. The gesture gave her great comfort, and she turned to smile at him. As Peter finally led her toward the door to leave, Sara stopped one last time and turned to Dr. Pearlman.

"What happened to him? The man who raped her?"

"He was arrested for war crimes shortly after the war ended. I'm told he tried to escape and was shot and killed." The doctor paused and added, "It was too easy an ending for him. He deserved much worse."

Sara nodded and followed Peter out the door.

Twenty-One

PETER'S ARM RESTED across Sara's shoulder and stayed there for the entire walk back to the inn, as if he wanted to steady her, reassure her, show her that he cared. Sara didn't say a word to him, and she didn't need to; he understood and respected her silence. But in her head there raged a loud conversation. Everything she had come to understand about her beginnings had suddenly been turned upside down, now even more than before. She was struggling to make sense of what Dr. Pearlman—her grandfather—had just told her. And the buzz inside her head all boiled down to one question that echoed like a broken record: What now? What now? What now? That morning, she'd been clear about her need to get out of Germany and return to Canada. Now she wasn't so sure what she should do.

When Peter and Sara walked into the inn, they found Frau Klein seated in a chair in the living room. At first, Sara feared that something might have happened to her. Why else would she be here and not bustling around the inn as she usually did? Why was she not preparing something for her and Peter to eat?

Sara rushed to her side and bent to look into her face. But Frau Klein was not ill or upset. In her lap was a small wiggling mass wrapped in a wool blanket. And when Sara looked closer, she realized that the bundle contained a tiny puppy.

"Oh, how wonderful," Sara exclaimed, dropping to her knees next to Frau Klein. "Wherever did it come from?" For a moment, her own startling situation was put on hold.

Frau Klein said something to Peter, who translated. "One of her neighbors has a dog that had puppies a few weeks ago. They worried it might be too soon for Frau Klein to have a new dog. But as soon as they saw this one, they knew that it needed a home right here."

Sara leaned forward toward the little pup while Peter continued talking to Frau Klein. It was a miniature John Wayne—a black-and-white, short-haired mongrel with the biggest and most trusting eyes that Sara had ever seen.

Peter suddenly laughed. "Frau Klein has named this one Roy Rogers. She can't seem to get away from her love of American westerns."

Sara bent her face toward the puppy. "Hello, Roy Rogers. You've got big shoes to fill, my little friend." The dog extended his face toward Sara and licked her cheek. Sara buried her face in his fur.

Just then there was a knock at the door. Peter went to answer it while Sara remained with Frau Klein, cooing over the puppy and stroking his soft fur. Frau Klein continued to smile and talk in German to the little dog. A moment later, Peter returned with an envelope in his hands. He had a frown on his face as he extended it to Sara. "It's for you," he said. "Who else do you know here?"

Sara shook her head. "I can't imagine who it's from." She took the envelope and turned it over in her hands. The return address on the back read *International Tracing Service, Bad Arolsen*. Dread rose up inside of her. She didn't want anything to do with that terrible place.

"Are you going to open it or just stare at it?" Peter had asked a similar question at the center, when she found her mother's file. She tore open the brown envelope. A letter fell out, and Sara picked it up.

"It's from Frau Kaufmann," she said. "The woman in the records room."

She looked up at Peter, whose face was urging her to read it. With a quick breath, she began to read aloud.

Dear Sara,

I've been sick with worry ever since you ran from my office. I was terribly sorry to have been the one who gave you the information about how you were conceived. It's not what I had wanted to do. But more important, it's not what your mother would have wanted for you. You asked when you were here what kind of person she was. And I believe that I owe you that information. Your mother was one of the kindest and most generous women I ever met. One day I watched her help another woman in the concentration camp carry food to a work site. It was against the regulations to help another prisoner, but your mother didn't care about the risk to herself. One of the guards noticed, came over and struck your mother in the back with his rifle butt. She could have been killed. But she just got up off the ground and continued to help. And that was just one incident. There are many more examples of the way in which she reached out to help others.

Sara paused and looked up. "I just wish that I could have known her."

"She seems like a remarkable person," Peter replied.

Sara nodded and continued to read.

You ran out of the office before I could give you something. I think you need to have this—a reminder of the wonderful woman that was your mother.

"What's inside?" Peter asked.

Sara shook the envelope, and a picture floated out and dropped to the floor. When Sara picked it up, she realized it was the photo of her mother that she had found in the file in the records room. Sara stared down at the face that looked so much like her own.

"Is that everything?" Peter asked.

"No, there's a bit more."

Your mother had many ambitions that she was unable to fulfill. When we were recovering together in Föhrenwald, she learned how to sew. It was part of a vocational program that was offered there. Your mother was very good at it—a natural—and she created some wonderful dresses and skirts. She dreamed that one day she would become someone famous in the world of clothing and fashion. Sadly, she was never able to fulfill that dream.

Sara looked up once more, eyes shining. "She wanted to be a designer," she said, breathless. "I can't believe what I'm reading."

"I guess there's more of your mother in you than you thought," Peter said.

Sara looked down at the photo of her mother and then picked up Frau Kaufmann's letter to read the last segment.

There is so much tragedy that befell your mother—tragedy that you also have to bear. But take the little that you know of this remarkable woman's life and be inspired by it. It was a gift to have known her.

I wish you well as you go forward in your life.

Warm regards,

Hedda Kaufmann

Little Roy Rogers yapped and licked at the tears that were falling down Sara's cheeks. She held the letter from Frau Kaufmann in one hand and the photograph of her mother in the other, shifting her gaze back and forth between the two. After what felt like minutes, Peter cleared his throat and spoke.

"What now?" he asked.

Sara looked up, tears still streaming, and said, "I think there's one more place I have to go to."

Twenty-Two

SARA AND PETER stood facing the wrought-iron gate that was the entrance to the Jewish cemetery in Gauting. A large Star of David adorned the top of the gate. Sara's conversation with Peter about coming here had been brief. In fact, there had barely been any conversation at all. He understood immediately her need to visit this place and had quickly gone about getting information about the train schedule and directions. It had not been hard to find. The train from Wolfratshausen had taken just over an hour. Then they had hitched a ride with a quiet couple who knew exactly where the cemetery was. And here they were, standing silently in front of the gate.

Sara gazed up at the large Star of David and quietly fingered the smaller one around her neck. After reading the letter from Frau Kaufmann, she already knew that she was connected to her mother in a deep and personal way. And yet there was something more she yearned for. She couldn't quite explain what it was. But in her heart, she believed that standing in front of her mother's grave would give her the resolution she was looking for.

Peter turned to Sara, waiting for her cue. When she nodded slightly, he approached the gate and pulled on it. "It's locked," he said, turning back to stare at Sara.

She tried not to show her dismay as she looked around. There was no one in sight—no visitors, no groundskeeper, no one. Why were these things always so complicated, Sara wondered, glancing up at the long stone wall that extended on both sides of the gate. Her mind drifted back to the orphanage in Hope. She had a sudden image of Joe standing next to her, prodding her to finish a project or get on with her chores. He would have smiled that great warm smile, and he would have said, *Now Sara, you know that nothin' in life worth fightin' for comes easy*. He had always been so wise. If need be, Sara would scale the wall—whatever she had to do to get inside. Peter stepped in before she had a chance to start climbing.

"I know you can't wait to get in. But let's just walk around first and see if there's another way."

Sara could barely contain her impatience. But she knew Peter was being reasonable. She followed him to the end of the brick wall, and as they rounded the bend, they realized that the brick wall and gate were merely at the front of the cemetery. It appeared to be enclosed on the other three sides with a high hedge of bushes.

"Much better," said Peter. "We just need to find a gap and we'll crawl through."

They'd walked about halfway around the exterior before they found the opening they were searching for. The bushes here were thinner and spaced farther apart. Peter held the branches of one of them back while Sara slipped in between and into the interior of the cemetery. Then she turned and did the same for him. Finally, they were inside.

Small white gravestones dotted the green field of the cemetery. The writing on all of them was in German, sometimes in Hebrew, but she could read the names: Solomon, Goldman, Feinberg...Sara walked between the gravestones, pausing every now and then to stare at a particular one. The dates indicated that most of the people buried here had died in the year or two following the end of the Second World War. It was not hard to understand how they, like her mother, had somehow survived the concentration camps only to succumb in the years after. There was a huge monument in the center of the park. It too had a large Star of David carved on top. The number 6,000,000 had been engraved in the center of the stone—the number of Jews who had perished in the Holocaust. Sara shuddered, and Peter moved over to wrap his arm around her shoulder. His lips brushed the top of her head, and she smiled up at him, taking strength from his embrace.

Dr. Pearlman had given them instructions for where to find Sara's mother's grave, and they followed them along a twisting path, turning this way and that, down a small hill, then turning once again to the right and then to the left.

"I'm amazed at how well kept this place is," Sara remarked. Up until then, neither of them had spoken a word. The graves were pristine, and the grass in between was thick and lush. The stone path was in perfect condition.

"I don't even know who takes care of it," Peter replied. "I imagine the Jewish families of this area contribute money to maintain it. Perhaps the government also helps. But I'm also surprised by its condition. I know that there are Jewish cemeteries all over Europe where the graves have been vandalized, and the stones knocked over and destroyed."

Sara felt a deep sense of gratitude that this cemetery was so well cared for. She didn't know how she would have reacted if her mother's grave had been damaged.

On and on they walked, moving deeper into the cemetery. They finally rounded one more turn and there it was, right in front of them. The white stone read *Karen Frankel, 1925–1946*. There was some German writing engraved below the name.

"What does it say?" Sara was breathless, barely able to get the question out.

"It says *Beloved Daughter, Wife and*"—Peter paused and looked up—"*Mother.*"

The word *mother* took Sara's breath away again. Her mother lay here in the earth—just bones and dust now. But Sara felt close to her for the first time in her life. As she stood and stared at the grave, she was suddenly aware that Peter had come up behind her and once again slipped his arm around her shoulders.

"It's so hard to explain why I needed to come here," Sara finally said.

"People usually don't need a reason to visit a grave. They come to pay their respects and to remember."

"But that's just it. I have no memories of her, just things I've invented, or the few things that people like Frau Kaufmann and Dr. Pearlman have told me."

She still couldn't call him grandfather. "Those are their memories, not mine."

They stood in silence for a few moments, and then Sara began to talk again.

"But it is pretty here," she said, looking up at the trees that hung protectively over the gravestones and squinting at the sun that was peeking through the taller branches. "I guess I'm grateful that she's here in this peaceful place."

Sara could feel a sense of calm and peace moving throughout her body. It was as if all the anxiety, irritation, insecurity and uncertainty of her life was being released as she stood here. Her arms rested at her sides. Her hands were still. This was a new feeling, a good feeling. She wanted it to last.

"I wish I had some flowers to put on her grave." Tears flowed freely down Sara's cheeks now, and she did not try to stop them.

Peter looked around and picked up a small round stone. "Jews don't usually bring flowers to a cemetery," he said. "Instead, we place stones on a grave."

Sara paused. "It seems so harsh." Flowers would have been so much nicer, so much prettier, she thought.

"Well, flowers disappear quickly. The belief is that stones last forever, just like the memory you hold of the one who has died." Peter held the stone out to Sara.

She took it, turning it over in her hand. Then she approached the grave and laid the stone on top of the marker, letting her hand rest there for a moment. She liked this custom. Perhaps she had no old memories of her mother, but starting right now, she could create a new memory of this moment, one that would last into the future. Then she stepped back and stared at her mother's grave.

Everything was becoming clearer to her. Yes, she would carry the man who had raped her mother somewhere inside of her. Every time she looked into a mirror, stared at her blue eyes, she would be reminded of her roots. But she knew now that she was not him, and never would be. She would live her life trying to prove that. And she would start by fulfilling her mother's destiny. She would become the designer her mother had never been able to become. She would study—somehow, somewhere—and she would keep the pact that she had made with Dot.

The question *What now?* had been raging in Sara's head for the last couple of days. But she was startled to realize that she was experiencing an odd sense of belonging here, as if in standing at her mother's grave she suddenly sensed that Germany was a place where she might fit in—more than she had ever fit in at the orphanage. Perhaps her destiny was here, if only for the next little while. She had a grandfather—a blood relative—with whom she needed to try to create a relationship. And then there was Peter. Was there something there? Perhaps. It was definitely worth staying and seeing what would happen.

Sara's brain was in overdrive. She had some money left to live on—what was left of her nest egg. Maybe some of it might even go to helping support the upkeep of this cemetery and her mother's grave. She would need to talk to Peter about that.

Frau Klein might be able to use her help at the inn in exchange for room and board. Peter had said that the inn would get a lot busier as summer approached, and Sara already felt close to and comfortable with Frau Klein. She knew that the elderly woman felt the same toward her. *Everyone's substitute grandmother*, Peter had said. Perhaps Frau Klein would become more than a substitute to her. And then there was that sewing room at the back of the inn. Frau Klein had made it clear that Sara was welcome to use it any time. It was summoning her as if it had some magic power.

She suddenly felt an intense desire to write to Dot and tell her all of this. Maybe she'd even write to Malou, explaining what it felt like to finally feel at peace with who you were. She would definitely send a letter off to Mrs. Hazelton, who she knew would be happy at her decision to remain in Germany a while longer.

At the thought of Mrs. Hazelton, Sara paused. The matron had told her that she needed to look back and explore her past in order to understand herself. Well, she had done enough of that—had discovered everything that she needed to know. Now Sara knew that it was time to look forward. She grabbed Peter's hand and held it tightly. Then the two of them turned to leave the cemetery.

This time, Sara did not look back.

AUTHOR'S NOTE

Although *Stones on a Grave* is a work of fiction, there are some historical elements of this story that are true.

In the aftermath of the Holocaust, many survivors of the Nazi concentration camps were left homeless, malnourished and extremely sick. The United Nations Relief and Rehabilitation Administration (UNRRA) was assigned responsibility for these sick and displaced refugees. A number of former concentration camps became the home for these individuals and became known as displaced persons (DP) camps. Föhrenwald was the largest of these DP camps. It grew to have nearly 5,000 people and developed a rich educational and cultural life. It had a school, vocational training institute and religious academy, and it provided music and theater for its residents.

By 1950 most inhabitants of Föhrenwald had found new homes elsewhere. The camp finally closed in 1957. Since then it has been renamed Waldram and has become a residential neighborhood.

Bad Arolsen is the home of the International Tracing Service, an organization that collects the records of the millions who were persecuted under the Nazi regime. These archives were only opened to the public in 2007.

ACKNOWLEDGMENTS

Huge thanks to Eric Walters, who was the inspiration behind the original Seven series and then developed the idea of giving voice to seven female characters. Your creativity never ceases to amaze me. I'm thrilled to be on this ride and grateful to be able to bring my personal commitment to telling stories of the Holocaust to this project. Thanks as well to Teresa Toten, our navigator and guiding spirit, and to the other writers in this series. I'm proud to be in your company. I'm indebted to Andrew Wooldridge and all the folks at Orca for making this series possible. Special thanks to Sarah Harvey for her encouragement and watchful eye on all of these stories. Thanks as well to Katrin Farkas for the German translations. And to my personal readers, Ian, Jake, Gabi, Rose and Ness, I value your support and feedback more than you can know.

KATHY KACER is the author of many books for young readers, including *The Secret of Gabi's Dresser*, *Clara's War*, *The Underground Reporters*, *Hiding Edith*, *The Diary of Laura's Twin*, *To Hope and Back*, *Shanghai Escape* and, her latest book, *The Magician of Auschwitz*. A winner of the Silver Birch, Red Maple, Hackmatack and Jewish Book Awards in Canada and the United States, as well as the Yad Vashem award for Children's Holocaust Literature in Israel, Kathy has written unforgettable stories inspired by real events. Her books have been translated into more than twenty languages and sold to Germany, China, Italy, Thailand, England, Japan, Korea, Israel, Brazil, Belgium and many other countries. Her novels are stories of hope, courage and humanity in the face of overwhelming adversity.

Although she has been writing for many years, Kathy only became a published author in 1999. Before that, she worked as a psychologist with troubled teens. Kathy teaches writing at the University of Toronto's School of Continuing Studies. She also speaks to children and educators in schools and libraries around the world about the importance of understanding the Holocaust and keeping its memory alive. For more information, visit www.kathykacer.com.

Uncover more Secrets—
starting with this excerpt from:

I WAS ALMOST back to my cabin when Glennie stepped out of the Harem. The light above the door made her curlers sparkle. She had a pink cosmetic kit, slightly smaller than your average hockey bag, tucked under her arm.

"Oh, hey!" she said, bouncing over. "I've been thinking about you. What's your name again?"

"Dot."

"Right. Dot. I realize forgetting your name makes me sound somewhat insincere about wanting to see you—but banish that thought. Just the way I am. Slightly scatterbrained. All part of my enormous charm." She took a bobby pin out of her hair and opened it with her teeth. "So what have you been up to?"

And because she was there and Sara wasn't, I said, "I've been out with Eddie Nicholson."

"I heard that from one of the dock boys—and he wasn't too thrilled about it, I must say. Too bad. If Finlay wanted you, he should've moved faster. I told him that." She rammed the bobby pin through a curler, almost dropping her cosmetic bag in the process. "Isn't Eddie a charmer?"

My shoulders squeezed into my neck with the utter thrill of it. "Yes."

"Did he take you for lunch in Hidden Bay?"

I nodded.

"In some swish boat?"

"Really nice boat."

"Probably Ward's. And then back to that cottage of his?"

I nodded again.

"Isn't it appalling? But what can you do? *Maman est disparue* and papa as good as. But you no doubt heard all about that. Gunky's 'bad' war, the leg blown to smithereens at—insert name of battle here—the subsequent drinking..."

"Gunky?" I said. "That's his father's name?"

"That's what they call him. Must be short for Gordon or Gunga Din or something. I don't know. Anyway"—she flapped a hand in front of her like a puppy begging—"that's not what I wanted to talk to you about. I've been terrible, ignoring you like this. High time you got to know some of the youngsters around here—so I'm taking you to the Bye-Bye Baby party. And PS, Finlay will be there."

"Who's Finlay?"

"Finlay? Finlay Hart. The dock boy I told you about. Black hair. Imposing physique. Old money. He was ogling you from the dock today. You didn't notice?"

"No."

"Oh, he'll be livid. Finlay is used to being noticed. So—Bye-Bye Baby? You're on?"

"Ahh. When is it?" I'd never been to a party before.

"The Wednesday after next. Be there or be square, as they say."

This was the party Eddie'd been talking about. I didn't want to go. Not with all those strangers. It made me feel slightly sick. "I've got a lot of work to do. Mrs. Smees doesn't—"

"You clearly don't know what Bye-Bye Baby is."

I put on an awkward semi-smile while I tried to come up with an answer.

"I knew it. Bye-Bye Baby—Triple B, if you will—is the annual commemoration of a bizarre occurrence that took place right here seventeen years ago."

She looped her arm through mine. "Picture this. A girl and a boy. In the woods. After curfew. Doing the type of things hot-blooded teens are known to do after curfew. At some point in the proceedings, they come up for air, only to discover a baby.

Lying on the ground." She paused for effect. "A tiny, blood-soaked newborn baby." She held up her hand. "No bigger than this."

My jaw fell. My eyes popped.

"Oooh. What a gratifying reaction."

"What happened to the baby?"

"That's the thing. That's why July 8, 1947, shall live on in infamy. The couple was understandably concerned to find a defenseless infant left in the woods. I mean, who knows what could have happened? A wild animal could have raised it as its own. One of the guests' Yorkies could have trotted down to the patio with its tiny lifeless body clamped between its jaws. You can imagine how terrible that would be for business. So, being good Dunbrae employees, they attempted to rescue the child. They reached over to pick it up and—poof!"

I jumped.

"The baby disappeared right before their eyes. Now we honor this momentous occasion every year by returning to that very same spot and doing what those employees did so long ago: drinking ourselves stupid. I'd hate for you to miss it."

She went on for a while in that same vein, then must have headed to the staff washroom. I don't remember. I stood alone in the courtyard of the colony, my head buzzing.

An unusually tiny baby.

Born the very day I was born.

The mysterious disappearance.

The coat.

The Buckminster address.

I stumbled back to my cabin in a fog. I stood on the step to unlock the door and something crunched beneath my shoe. I flicked it away with my foot, figuring it was just a twig. I was too rattled by Glennie's story to check.

I realize now, of course, it was probably the first of the bones.

"What's this?"

Mrs. Smees spilled a pile of floral silk onto my table, then stood back, arms crossed, squinting at me.

"That's Mrs. Illsley's dress. I—"

"I know what it is. I just don't know why you'd call it fixed." She pulled a pencil out of her hair and poked at the dress. "That seam look fixed to you? Think that's enough to keep them big hips of hers from busting out all over the family pew when she kneels down at St. Ninian's this Sunday?"

"Oh. No, I must have just missed it. I—"

"Missed? I'm not paying you to *miss* things. My guess is you're spending more time thinking about our young Mr. Nicholson than you are about your job."

She was only partly right about Eddie. I'd barely slept the night before. I couldn't get that story about the baby out of my head.

It couldn't have been true. It was just a creepy story. A creepy made-up story like the ones Patsy used to tell us about the ghost of Mrs. Hazelton's dead (and usually naked) lover roaming the halls of the Home every full moon and calling, calling, calling her name. We'd all scream and huddle together and make someone come to the bathroom with us for weeks afterward, despite knowing full well she'd concocted the whole thing. (Mrs. Hazelton with a lover? Even I couldn't swallow that one.)

This was the same. I knew the story had to be nonsense, but I still couldn't shake it. I'd tossed and turned all night, trying to make sense of it. All these years fantasizing about where I'd come from, I'd never considered anything mystical about my background. The parents I'd dreamed up may have been implausible, but they'd always been human.

Now two tiny babies, two mysteries, same date, both linked to Buckminster. Hard not to entertain the idea that there was some connection. The disappearing-before-their-very-eyes thing just kind of ruled out a human one. I wondered if the ladies' auxiliary was going to tell me the spoon came from a witch's coven or something.

I had another go at Mrs. Illsley's dress and was careful to make sure everything was perfect this time. I just prayed Mr. Oliphant would hold off telling Mrs. Smees about the coffee incident until I was back in her good books again. I didn't need two strikes against me.

I ate a sandwich at my table at lunchtime and didn't take a break until Mrs. Smees said, "It's quarter to six. Get going. Don't hang around here, expecting me to pay you overtime."

By the time I got to the colony, other kids were already there. Dock boys shooting their balled-up Dunbrae shirts into a hoop nailed to the side of the Meat Department, waitresses laughing and whispering on the steps of the Harem. I didn't want to run into them. I slid in along the hedge to my cabin, then jumped back, hand over mouth.

Eddie was sitting on the steps behind the lilac bushes.

"You. Scared. Me."

"Sorry. Didn't mean to—which isn't to say I didn't enjoy it immensely."

"Did I do that toad thing again?"

"Toad? You? I have no idea of what you speak." He patted the steps and slid over to make room next to him.

"What's that in your hand?" I said.

He shrugged. "The remains of a bird, by the looks of it." He tossed the bones into the bushes. "So, can I drag you out tonight? Take you to the falls maybe. You like fishing?"

"Yeah, I do. I'd really love to, but—" I couldn't screw up at work again. I couldn't lose my job. "I think I should just go to bed. Mrs. Smees got mad at me today."

"That's news?"

"Well, yeah. This time I deserved it. I was sloppy. Too tired, I guess. Didn't sleep well last night."

He leaned down and pulled my foot onto his knee. "How come?" He tied my shoe for me, then put it back down.

"Bad dreams," I managed to say.

"Smees dreams?"

"No. I ran into Glennie after you took me home. She told me this ghost story, and I don't know, it just kind of spooked me."

"Excellent. I love ghost stories. Unburden yourself." He bumped elbows with me, and the hairs on my arm all reached out for him. "Tell me."

"You probably know it already. Bye-Bye Baby? Silly."

"That's not a ghost story. That actually happened."

I looked at him out of the corner of my eye.

"I'm not kidding." He raised his hand. "Scout's honor."

"A baby disappeared into thin air?"

"Well, okay. That part's made up, but the rest is true."

"How do you know? You wouldn't have been around. You're too young."

"My babysitter."

"You have a babysitter? Big boy like you?"

The elbow again. "When I was a kid, I mean. After Mum left. Dad needed someone to look after me while he was working. This college girl helped out. Sandra Smithers. She's Conway now. Anyway, I heard her talking about the Bye-Bye Baby party one day with her friends—this would have been five or six years later, I guess—and I asked her what it was. That was the great thing about Sandra. You were cute enough, she'd tell you anything."

"And? What'd she say?"

He leaned back, his elbows on the step behind him, legs out straight like hockey sticks. Deck shoes. No socks.

"I thought you were tired," he said.

"Not that tired."

"Okay. Well. That area back there?" He leaned around the lilac bush and pointed to the woods beyond the colony. "I mean, way back. Good ten-, fifteen-minute walk. There's a clearing. Kids have had their parties there forever. Dad said they even did in his day. Anyway, that night a bunch of kids go up as per usual. Somewhere toward midnight, this couple goes off on their own and they hear a noise. At first they think it's an animal. Maybe it's been hurt or something, so they go to look and find this, like, minuscule baby just lying on the ground."

"That's pretty much what Glennie told me."

"Yeah. But here's where it gets different. Story they tell now is that the baby vanished before their very eyes, right? *Ripley's Believe It or Not!* stuff. That's not what Sandra said. She said the kids left the baby to get help. She was the first person they found, so the three of them raced back. By the time they got there, the baby was gone. Someone had taken it."

"Taken it?"

"Yeah."

"Who?"

"Beats me."

"Where was the mother?"

He shrugged. "No sign of anyone. No one's ever figured out how it got there."

"What happened to the baby?"

"Ditto. No clue. Mention it now and everyone acts like it's a myth or something. As if you're asking what happened to Snow White or the tooth fairy."

We sat on the steps, quiet for a while. Me thinking—more like *believing* in that you-just-know kind of way—that this was my story. That there might actually be a rational explanation after all. I didn't know what the explanation was yet, of course, or how I was going to go about finding it.

And then suddenly, I just did.

"You should do a story on it," I said. "For the paper."

Eddie turned and looked at me. "I was thinking the exact same thing."

"Eerie, isn't it?" Our little joke, but he didn't laugh.

"It is." He was sitting up now, kind of twitchy through the shoulders, eyes sparkly. "Make a great article. Everyone around here has heard the rumors. Maybe it's time the real story came out."

"Where are you going to get that?"

He rolled out his bottom lip and thought. "So this happened in 1948..."

"In '47. At least, according to Glennie."

"Right—'47. The *Gleaner* may have done something on it then, though not if it just looked like a bunch of kids making up stories. Still, there might be some clues there. I'll check the office, see if they have issues going back that far. There's also the resort's reading room."

"What is that anyway? Mrs. Smees wanted me to go there the other day."

"It's like a library. Books, magazines, that type of thing, but they also keep photos and newspaper clippings about anything connected to the Arms."

"Such as?"

"I don't know. Weddings, funerals, obits, not to mention endless stories about dock boys getting accepted at Yale or Mrs. So-and-So the Third hosting her much-anticipated annual garden party. Could be something there."

He put his hands behind his neck, looked at the sky, then shook his head. "You know what though? I doubt it. A missing baby? Not the type of story the Arms likes to remember. They'd be more likely to cover it up. Not sure where else to look."

"What about your babysitter? She still around?"

He gawked at me. I thought I'd said something wrong.

"Sandra. Of course. I even ran into her last week. She asked if I'd pop by her cottage. She's got some sort of rodent problem. Want to come—or you too tired?"

He laughed when I said no girl could resist a boy with a rodent problem.

EVERY FAMILY HAS A SKELETON IN THE CLOSET...

Are you ready for more Secrets?

THE UNQUIET PAST

KELLEY ARMSTRONG

9781459806542 pb
9781459806573 pdf
9781459806580 epub

SMALL BONES

VICKI GRANT

9781459806535 pb
9781459806566 pdf
9781459806559 epub

A BIG DOSE OF LUCKY

MARTHE JOCELYN

9781459806689 pb
9781459806696 pdf
9781459806702 epub

SECRETS

STONES ON A GRAVE

KATHY KACER

9781459806597 pb
9781459806603 pdf
9781459806610 epub

MY LIFE BEFORE ME

NORAH MCCLINTOCK

9781459806627 pb
9781459806634 pdf
9781459806641 epub

SHATTERED GLASS

TERESA TOTEN

9781459806719 pb
9781459806726 pdf
9781459806733 epub

INNOCENT

ERIC WALTERS

9781459806658 pb
9781459806665 pdf
9781459806672 epub

THE SECRETS BOXED SET

9781459810822 pb
9781459810839 pdf
9781459810846 epub

Read the Secrets in any order.

Also available as audio!

www.**readthesecrets**.com